W.T.E. . . .

Athena stood there, robes blowing in the stiff, warm breeze, and tilted her helmeted head back. "Come to me, Bellerophon's steed. Come to me, Pegasus, and bring your brood!"

I grabbed his arm and pointed upward. At first it might have been a flock of seagulls, white against blue. But the illusion that they were birds disappeared as they neared. They were horses, all right. White horses with great big feathered white wings.

"Well, I know I should be tired of saying this by now, but that is just impossible," Jalil said, sounding disgusted. "You cannot lift a horse into the air with bird wings. And how does it turn? It has a horse tail not feathers. It couldn't turn. But it does."

"W.T.E.," David said.

"Yes, Welcome to Everworld, I know," Jalil grumbled.

Four flying horses swooped down toward us, hooves tucked, tails flapping idly with the wind, heads held high without regard to aerodynamics, wings slowly beating.

Had I ever see anything more beautiful? Had I ever in my life, here in Everworld, or my real life back in the world, had I ever anything to compare? It made me want to cry for a universe where no such creature existed or could exist. . . .

Look for other EVERWORLD titles

by K.A. Applegate:

EVER WORLD

GATEWAY TO THE GODS

K. A. APPLEGATE

SCHOLASTIC INC.
New York Toronto London Auckland Sydney
Mexico City New Delhi Hong Kong

No part of this publication may be reproduced in whole or in part, or stored in a retrieval system, or transmitted in any form or by any means, electronic, mechanical, photocopying, recording, or otherwise, without written permission of the publisher. For information regarding permission, write to Scholastic Inc., Attention: Permissions Department, 555 Broadway, New York, NY 10012.

ISBN 0-590-87766-6

12 11 10 9 8 7 6 5 4 3 2   3 4 5/0

Printed in the U.S.A.

First Scholastic printing, May 2000

FOR MICHAEL AND JAKE

GATEWAY TO THE GODS

CHAPTER
I

Olympus.

Let me just say this: After all the filth, the fleas, the mud, the hunger, the burning thirst, the never, never, never any decent sleep, this was all right.

This was more than all right. This was the Everworld Ritz-Carlton. This was the Four Seasons Everworld. This was Club Everworld.

And once you made it really clear, several times, that no, you really, actually, for sure did not want a glass of wine, or mead, or ale; and no, you honestly didn't want the "services" of a young handsome god, an old lecher god, an effeminate god, a macho god, a god disguised as a bull, an eagle, a ram, a horse, for crying out loud, or a goat, but would really, really, actually rather just sleep, it was quite enjoyable.

They had beds that ... how can I even describe these beds? To say that they were deep clouds of the softest down wrapped in some magical fabric that was as smooth and cool as silk but with the comfort of 300-count Egyptian cotton doesn't begin to touch the profound, soul-soothing wonder of the experience.

I had slept on the ground for a long time. To go from dirt, with a probable tree root stabbing me in the back, to this ... I mean, it was only the Greek pagan version of heaven, not the real thing, but it would do. It would definitely do. Saint Peter would have to hustle to impress me after this.

Breakfast was served by the inevitably underclothed pretty young thing — male in this case. It was a silver platter roughly the length and depth of a library table, loaded with red-flesh oranges, green and pink and red apples, pale red cherries, split green and orange melons, and six different types of grapes.

Then there were the breads: flat bread, braided bread, wheat bread, white bread in the shape of a mushroom with seeds on top. And, of course, the cakes: cakes made with honey and poppy seeds and currants, some shaped like crescents, some shaped like little shoes filled with cream cheese, some shaped like parts of the female anatomy you don't normally expect to find staring up at you from your breakfast tray.

Eggs? Of course there were eggs: from chickens, from ducks, from geese, from robins and eagles and hummingbirds — very tiny.

Then there were the distinctly Mediterranean touches: olives, maybe six kinds, ranging from almost sweet to intensely salty; raw clams and raw oysters and steamed mussels and shrimp you could saddle up and ride and chunks of white fish sizzling hot on silver skewers.

In addition to each of these dishes there were little pottery bowls filled with six different kinds of honey, two different butters, various creams, an array of cheeses made from goat's milk, cow's milk, sheep's milk, and yes, unicorn's milk.

Unicorn-milk cheese. This is something you seldom see on even the finest menus in Chicagoland.

Woven through and around the food itself were the garnishes and decorations: the flowers, the sprigs of herbs, the decorative swirls of gold thread wrapped into little pagan idols.

And every single thing, every single cake, every single loaf of bread, every dollop of cream, every last grape on every last bunch was perfect. It wasn't "a" strawberry, it was "the" strawberry. The oranges were so good I cried.

It was enough food to feed me for three weeks. And it was just breakfast.

We had spent the night before in Olympus. I had bathed in hot, hot, clean water in a marble bath so big I could have swum laps. I had traded my verminous, stiff-with-filth rags for an elegant dress that was slit up both sides but was otherwise pretty prim by Olympus's standards. I had enjoyed a dinner so extravagant, so wonderful that Charlie Trotter and Wolfgang Puck and that Emeril guy on TV would have had to retire after witnessing its unattainable perfection. I had enjoyed a fabulous night's fabulous sleep. And now I had eaten a breakfast that could have fueled the entire Chicago marathon.

I wanted nothing more than to escape Everworld permanently. To get back home. But maybe not right this minute.

A knock at my door.

"Yes?" I said, filled to bubbling over with goodwill for all creatures big and small.

The door opened. Christopher stood there, wearing a toga.

"I just have one question for you," he said. "Is this place cool or what?"

"Did you get breakfast?" I asked eagerly.

"No. No, I didn't get breakfast. I got an entire brunch buffet table. You can't even call it breakfast. That would be an insult. It was BREAKFAST in giant, flaming Hollywood-sign letters a hundred feet tall. Damn, these people run a great hotel."

I grinned. He grinned. Jalil poked his head around the corner and he was grinning. There are few pleasures in life deeper than the pleasure of a filthy, thirsty, hungry, tired human being who gets a hot bath, a cold drink, a great meal, and ten hours of deep untroubled sleep. (Although in truth I'd spent my "sleep" going to class, studying for a test, and heading for the old folks' home where I read Danielle Steel and Nora Roberts books to a couple of the women.)

"I just want to say this, right up front," Jalil said. "I'm not leaving. I'm never leaving. They will have to chase me out of here with a baseball bat, and even then, I'm not leaving."

"Where's David?" I asked.

Christopher shrugged. "I don't know, haven't seen him since last night at dinner. But I have a bet for you: I bet five bucks he can find some downside to all this."

I laughed. "No bet. That's too easy. You guys want some food? I have . . ." I looked at my breakfast tray, which looked as if it had never been touched. ". . . I think I have a few hundred thousand calories of goodies left."

"You have any of those poppy seed and honey cakes?" Jalil asked.

"Oh, aren't those good? Did you try them with that kind of off-white cream?"

The three of us sat perched on the side of my bed and ate some more, despite the fact that not ten minutes earlier I'd sworn I could never eat again.

David finally showed up after half an hour. He wore the standard-issue toga, his sword, and a look of dissatisfaction. Christopher and I both broke up and snorted our food.

"What's funny?" David demanded.

"Nothing," I said. "Want some food?"

"I've had plenty of food," he said. He sounded unhappy about that fact. "Plenty of food, plenty of juice, plenty of sleep. I'm even clean. But I can't seem to get any answers around this place. The servants are all like, 'I don't know, I am only here for your pleasure.' All they care about is feeding me and bringing me something to drink, and would I like a massage, and how about some soothing balm for my wounds and . . . you know." He raised his eyebrows suggestively. "Would I like whatever with whoever?"

"Damn them! That is intolerable!" Christopher mocked.

"Cute," David said.

"Massage?" I asked, considering the fact that my back was still sore from dragging around my backpack with our few minuscule possessions.

David nodded. "Yeah. Your choice of nymph or satyr. Or nymph and satyr. Or nymph, satyr, and a helot they call the Harsh Spartan. Don't ask. I did, and trust me, you don't want to know."

Christopher spread his hands wide, encompassing the marble and alabaster perfection of the room. "I am home. I mean, this place? Do you have any idea of the profit potential if we could book people from the real world in here? I mean, this is what, a five-thousand-dollar-a-night experience?"

"Extra for the Harsh Spartan," Jalil said.

Suddenly the door flew open. We jerked into readiness. David's sword was half drawn before we had a chance to see that it was a woman. Youngish, maybe thirty. Dark hair and dark eyes and both wild-looking.

She stood still, rolled her eyes upward, like she was having a seizure, and in a low moan intoned:

"Olympus by the Hetwan hordes besieged,
Hellas's gods Ka Anor shall feed,

Lest strangers bring the Witch to heed,
The alien blacksmith's secret need."

Having delivered that imperfect rhyme, she fluttered her eyes, then stared at us like we were the ones who had burst into her room.

"Who are you?" David demanded.

"I am Cassandra," the woman said.

"Oh, please," Jalil said. "Cassandra was the prophet, the, um, what are they called, the oracle. Yeah, Cassandra was the oracle who always spoke the truth but was cursed never to be believed."

"Yes," the woman said with an expression of petulant resignation replacing the wild-child look. "I know."

"So, wait," David said, frowning. "So she always speaks the truth, but no one believes her? So . . . so we should believe her. Right?"

"Do you believe her?" I asked.

David shook his head. "No."

"She's not Cassandra," Jalil said.

"How do you know?" Christopher demanded. "I mean, I know she isn't, but how do you know?"

That troubled Jalil. He scrunched his eyes and seemed to be trying to focus. "I don't . . . okay, wait, if she is then she just told us something valuable, right? Only what she told us was . . . was . . ."

"Was it haiku?" I wondered aloud. "Isn't haiku, like, seventeen syllables? So, it wasn't even haiku. Ha," I announced triumphantly, as though I had just worked out the grand unifying theory.

"What was it she said?" David asked. "I forget."

"What was it you said?" I asked the woman.

"Never mind," Cassandra said and walked away as abruptly as she had come.

"I think we just had an Everworld moment," Jalil said. "If we could remember what she said. And believe it . . ."

"Not worth remembering," Christopher said. "Because, you know, it was BS."

"Oh, yeah."

CHAPTER
II

Everworld.

A different universe. Not a different planet or a different place — an entirely different universe. This was a universe where magic was real. Where mythological figures were actual people. Where time didn't always plod along in the same old course. Where the laws of physics could be altered, if you had the power. Where everyone everywhere seemed to speak the same language.

I lived in two universes. Simultaneously? Not exactly. Time in Everworld and time in the real world were not in sync. They both seemed to be running forward but, for the Everworld me, it was as if the gears of time in the real world were slipping, jerking, sometimes racing ahead, other times moving along normally.

I, April O'Brien — the Everworld April

O'Brien — lived in Everworld. When I slept I, or at least my memories, slipped back across the universal divide and rejoined real-world April.

There are two of me. Except when Everworld me is asleep. Then there's only the real-world me. Although my Everworld body stays put in Everworld.

Confusing? Yes. Yes, very confusing. Which is me? Both. All of the above. I live a full and active life in the real world, hang out with my friends, go to school, do volunteer work, talk to my mom, kiss my dad when he gets home from work, drive around doing errands, practice my part in a play, do my homework, sleep, shower, eat . . . I remain as I always was.

Except for the fact that every now and then, at unpredictable moments, I get these sudden updates as the Everworld me comes crashing back in, filled with the latest news. News that is almost always bad.

I can be sitting in Blind Faith enjoying an order of bibim bop or lemon seitan or just a vegan carrot cake or whatever, gabbing away happily with my friends, and all of a sudden it's CNN: Breaking News! This just in: The other you, Everworld April, has just fallen asleep despite the fact that she's spent the last eight hours in a state of rigid terror and will probably die shortly.

Hi, April. How's it going? The other April is on a Viking ship on her way to try to kill an Aztec god who eats people's hearts. Have a nice day.

The images of horror . . . I can be on a date, getting ready for the Big Kiss, and suddenly into my unprepared brain flood images, impossibly fresh, terrifyingly real, of men in agony, of monsters, of horrors that the most evil mind could not dream up. Not like watching a movie. Not like reading about it. These are memories of real events, real things that happened to a real me. I can feel the pain. I can feel the sick fear.

It is eating away at real-world April, almost as much as it damages Everworld April. Maybe more. It's the real-world April I want to save. That's my life. That is my real life, and it is being poisoned by an onslaught of fear and rage.

And, too, more subtle, but almost as destructive in their own way, are the seductions of Everworld. The memories of beauty. The memories of excitement, of mad thrills, of independence and self-reliance, of impossible things done, and near misses survived. So I get all that, too. In my everyday world I suddenly realize that another me has stood up to a dragon, defied a god, been bold and brave. Another me is Indiana Jones.

I'm not one of those people who felt at odds with my world. I was comfortable in it. I was happy in it. Mostly. I have a place in the real world. I belong. I am happy belonging.

But Everworld is more. Brighter, louder, sweeter, and more harsh, stranger, more interesting, more challenging, so insanely dangerous, so terrifying. Just . . . so.

The friends I have in the real world are the core of my universe. My friends mean everything to me. I am of them, and they are part of me, and we will, I hope, be together forever, if not physically then emotionally, spiritually. We share hopes, we share interests, we share ambitions.

The friends I have in Everworld? Well, are David and Christopher and Jalil friends, exactly?

I sat watching them while they nibbled at my breakfast and argued over this and that. I was struck by how much I have come to know these three guys. How much I trusted them to varying degrees. And how sick of them I was, too. And how much they were shoving my own life aside.

We'd never been friends before. We'd been connected, but we hadn't known it. At school, back in the real world, my friends were mostly drama club. Mostly girls, some guys.

David and Christopher were guys I knew to say hi to, but nothing more. Jalil I knew a bit better, not much. Christopher and later David had both dated my half sister, Senna, but that didn't exactly recommend them to me. That didn't make me think they were guys I should be close to. More the opposite. If they liked Senna there had to be something seriously wrong with them.

And I was right. There was something wrong with David and with Christopher. But then, that's life, isn't it? Any interesting character has flaws. You learn that as an actor: It's not just the virtues but the flaws and weaknesses, even the twists and sicknesses and evils, that make an interesting role.

But knowing that didn't necessarily make these guys easy to get along with.

David was an attractive boy; I could see why Senna had chosen him. He wasn't an especially big guy. Average, you'd have to say. He had a dark Dylan McDermott thing going on, but less simian, also less handsome.

As far as I can judge, something went wrong in David's life at a fairly early age that makes him feel he needs to constantly prove himself. Maybe it's his dad, who is some kind of retired military officer. I don't know, and David isn't a person who talks about his feelings or his past.

Truth is, whatever it is that made David insecure and so desperately determined to prove himself strong and courageous, whatever that thing was, it worked to our advantage here in Everworld. Maybe all heroes, or at least a lot, have that same "gotta be a manly man" thing. Maybe, I don't know. Whatever. The fact is when things turn bad we turn to David and he accepts the burden.

It's unfair of us, especially me, because I know in my heart that David is trapped. He can't let himself fail, can't let himself run away and hide. He has to be brave and we all just kind of accept that and use that. There's something there that makes me feel kind of squeamish. Like putting an anorexic in charge of protecting a food stash, or hiring an obsessive-compulsive to clean your house. It works, but is it right?

Christopher is an easier person to like and an easier person to despise. He's charming, funny, laid-back, and utterly honest about his emotions. When Christopher is scared, you know it. When he's hungry or mad or resentful or horny or depressed, there's no hiding it.

He's bigger than David, blond and somewhere right between dopey-sweet and swaggering bully, depending on what's happening around him. Ninety percent of the time I like him.

The other ten percent of the time he's a sexist, racist, homophobic jerk.

I don't think he's happy; comics rarely are. He is funny. I know his throwback attitudes come from some weakness in him, some dark, sad place. I mean, racism isn't exactly a symptom of happiness and mental balance, is it?

To make matters worse, I'm afraid Christopher is either an alcoholic or heading down that path. From remarks he's made I know both his parents drink, probably too much.

And yet, I like him. Maybe that's wrong. Maybe I should just push him away, refuse to deal with his crap. But I can't. We're together in this, the four of us. Besides, there is hope for him. I think maybe there's real hope.

He was hurt by the death of Ganymede, Zeus's one boy toy among the many, many girl toys. Ganymede had saved Christopher's life. And Christopher had failed to save Ganymede. I think this had a very profound impact on Christopher. Why? I don't know for sure. Something about being stuck with a debt he could never repay. Anyway, that's what I picked up from the mutterings of his multiday drunken bender.

Then, finally, there's Jalil. Jalil the enigma. Jalil the impenetrable.

It's not a black–white thing, either. It's not that his skin is a different color than mine, or even that he is, I guess, smarter than me. Jalil is Teflon-coated. Armored. Camouflaged. You try and look inside him and your gaze is deflected. Your questions are turned aside. Your curiosity seems to slip and slide off him, leaving no trace. Is he hiding something? Or is he really just arrogant? Is he supremely insecure or supremely confident?

I don't know.

I like him, I trust him, I respect him. I used to think I was getting to know him, but that was self-deception on my part. He's subtler than I am, and I can't outwit him and somehow get inside him and reduce him to a few neat labels.

He scares me a little. I would never admit it to him. But he lives life without faith, without any recourse to any power other than his own. How can a person live in a world without any hope of God? It's like finding out that someone lives without ever eating. It fascinates me, it worries me, it makes me doubt myself.

There was, of course, one other person from the real world here with us in Everworld: Senna.

Senna is my half sister. We share a father. It seems my upright father was not always upright. He met Senna's mother. And some years later, Senna's mother simply disappeared. There were rumors that she was in this place or that, but never any proof.

So Senna came to live with us. With our father and my mother.

We hadn't seen Senna in a while. But she was

the reason we were here. She was the link between David, Jalil, Christopher, and me.

My feelings toward my companions were complicated. My feelings toward Senna were not.

I hated her.

CHAPTER

III

After another hour, they sent for us.

The servant, a very cute young man, a sort of Noah Wyle ten years ago, said, "You are to be honored by an audience with Great Zeus himself."

The servant seemed impressed. I felt the early warning signs of dread. We didn't know much about Everworld, about who was who, but we knew, at least we'd picked up, that Zeus was one of the founders. A major power. Someone to fear, despite the fact that we wanted him to survive.

"We're supposed to go see Zeus?" Jalil asked. "When?"

"As soon as you are ready."

Christopher said, "Shouldn't we just, you know, see, like, his secretary or something? His assistant?"

That drew a blank look from the servant. I had a more vital question.

"Hey, what do we wear? I mean, Zeus? That has to mean something formal. And what do we say to him? How do you, whatever they call it, how do you address him? What's his title?"

This the servant got. "Suitable clothing will be brought. You should address Great Zeus as Great Zeus, or Father of the Gods, or Lord of Olympus. Unless he should favor you with his divine attentions and take you to his bed, in which case you may wish to call him simply Zeus."

"Uh-huh." Great. One more reason to feel the tingle of anxiety.

"So basically, you don't want to be on a first-name basis with the Zeuster," Christopher observed. "Or maybe you do, April," he added, wiggling his eyebrows in what he no doubt thought was a suggestive way.

"Mmm, pretty sure I don't want my first time to be with a pagan god, Christopher. I have a feeling that my bringing that up at confession would pretty well kill Father Mike. Bad enough deciding what to do about that whole immortality thing."

Christopher, and possibly the rest of us as well, had been offered immortality for rescuing the god Dionysus from Ka Anor. I'd had the sense that the old drunk was leaving himself some wiggle room in his repeated assurances. But still, at least for Christopher, the offer was on the table.

Immortality. Live forever. Unless someone kills you. But no old age, no disease. Too big a thing to think about. Besides, it would only apply to the Everworld me, and I was hoping the Everworld me wouldn't be around long enough to benefit from immortality.

"Okay," David said, businesslike, to the servant. "If we need special clothes, bring them. If we need any special thing to say, you know, any kind of what do they call it? Um, you know, what's that word?" He snapped his fingers. "Etiquette. If there's any special etiquette, like we should bow or whatever, get someone to fill us in. We'll be ready ten minutes after you get us what we need."

The servant nodded and took off.

"David, you were made for snapping out orders to underlings," Jalil said dryly.

"Kind of makes you want to start calling him Massa Dave, eh, Jalil?" Christopher said.

Then he blushed.

The three of us stared. Partly in response to the crude humor. But more as we saw the blush. The notion of Christopher being embarrassed was new.

"Sorry," Christopher said shortly and turned away.

I don't know if he was mad at us or at himself,

or just looking to avoid yet another mass condemnation. But it was weird. Weird for Christopher.

The servant returned swiftly, along with an older woman. They were carrying new, classier togas for the men and a very cute dress for me: pale blue, ankle length, slit high up both sides, tied at the shoulders with gold threads, and forming a gathered neckline that swooped to a fairly chaste depth as long as I didn't bend over.

The woman also brought lace-up sandals. I refused and stuck with my sneakers. "Sorry, but superior footwear is about all we have going for us sometimes," I explained. She looked blank.

The truth was we had little of our original stuff left. But we still had our seldom-touched CD player, our blessed bottle of Advil, some money and keys, a book, a notepad that Jalil used to make maps and sketches, some fragments of our original clothing, and our assorted Nikes and New Balances. Thank God it had been an early morning when Senna drew us to the lake. Later in the day I might have slipped on a pair of boots. And here's a fact: You can flee for your life a whole lot quicker in running shoes than in boots.

Dressed, clean, fed, and feeling as well as I could under the circumstances, I rejoined the guys.

"Hey," Christopher said, "April's a girl!"

We all laughed at that. Then I said, "Yeah, but so are you all."

"Very funny," Jalil grumped. "I prefer not to think of it as a dress. I see it as more like a very baggy pair of shorts."

"Kilt?" David suggested. "You know, maybe a whole *Braveheart* thing?"

"Boys, you are wearing togas. And not long togas, either. I think we have ourselves a mini-toga look here. You're showing leg. You're showing knee and a few inches of thigh."

"Yeah, but we're gonna be immortal," Jalil said.

"Think the toga is part of the whole immortality deal?" David wondered.

"You know, about that whole thing, that whole immortal thing —" Christopher began.

He was interrupted by the arrival of the band. Yes, the band. Four guys playing a lute, a flute, a little drum, and a sort of horn like a cornet or a bugle.

"Oh, good, so it's not like anyone is going to notice us," Jalil said, shouting over the music.

The band led us out into the street. It was not paved with gold, but paved with marble that seemed to be veined with gold. It had the weird effect of making me think I was at the big downtown Marshall Fields.

The sky above was clear and blue. The air was marvelously clean and crisp, warm with no threat of hot. Unreal, too-perfect weather, unless you were from San Diego.

Along both sides of the marble street were buildings of granite and limestone and still more marble. Farther down the street the buildings grew more massive, with more and taller columns, but we were still among more modest houses. And by more modest I mean of course two or three times the size of one of those overblown new three-story suburban junior-vice-president homes.

Ahead the buildings grew exponentially. It caused a strange optical illusion. Things far away, though much the same in basic design, were six, eight, twelve, fifty times bigger than those nearby. It paradoxically made it seem that the street was very short. Not so.

"So we were stuck in the low-rent 'hood," Christopher complained. "Kind of humiliating, when you think about it. I mean, it was nice, but let's face it: We were in the Olympus Motel 6. And I kind of resent it."

The four-piece band walked ahead of us, riffing on a simpleminded theme of the sort that a musician might pick out on a piano while trying to come up with a really good idea.

It occurred to me that, gods or not, the people

who ran Olympus didn't know how to write music. Literally. No notes. No treble clefs.

We passed a fair number of strollers. Mostly they appeared to be pretty much human, although an unusually attractive, healthy, strong cross-section of humanity. But here and there would be glowing, seven- and even eight-foot-tall specimens that moved through the mortals like Kennedys among Kmart shoppers.

Olympus, at least this Everworld version of it, was a mountain sliced off neatly at the top. Like that mountain in *Close Encounters of the Third Kind*. Or like a volcano that's had its funnel paved over with gleaming stone.

It wasn't a city; it was too quiet and empty for that. And as far as I could tell, there was only this one wide avenue. It was almost a museum. A huge outdoor sculpture garden displaying the marvels of ancient Greek architecture.

It was a long walk from the Motel 6 to the neighborhood of the thoroughly magnificent. And my nerves started to work on me. Yes, we had rescued Dionysus, who, like a good two-thirds of the major gods, was a child of Zeus. So, in theory at least, we were welcome. But so far I was not impressed by the species of immortals.

We'd met immortal psychotics, killers, madmen, and madwomen. Not the people you want running your universe for you. And what we knew of Zeus from Dionysus's stories was that he liked to drink, liked to chase anything in a skirt, and would, when mad or plastered or just cranky, unleash a thunderbolt and kill people.

I also knew that Zeus's own personal home was the building at the end of the street. It was like the pictures you see of the Parthenon. Not all crumbled, but fresh and new. A double row of columns out front, peaked roof, stairs leading up, even a dome like Saint Peter's.

I had guessed that it was big. But after walking twenty minutes it was getting bigger still. Bigger and bigger.

It was bigger than the U.S. Capitol building. It was bigger than any building I'd ever seen. It was bigger than Aaron Spelling's house. Loki's entire castle could have been carried in the front doors.

What kind of creature lived in something like that? How did you remain humble when you owned a home like that?

"Well, April, I'm guessing humility is not a major virtue here," I muttered.

It felt as though we were shrinking. Like we had started out normal size but were now just about the size of ants. It was crushing.

We passed by a statue of a woman. She wore a helmet, like one of those Roman helmets you see when you channel surf past *Ben-Hur* on a Sunday afternoon.

The statue stood at the foot of a set of steps that rose maybe five stories. Atop the steps was a temple, not as large as that belonging to Zeus, but plenty big. This statue rose almost as high as the peak of the roof.

I gaped up at it. The feminist in me was obscurely pleased. I didn't know what role women had in this society, but whoever this woman was, she had R-E-S-P-E-C-T.

She wore a modest dress, not unlike mine. But she carried a huge oblong shield covering her left side. And in her right hand she carried a spear that she held up and out, jutting out over the street. A miracle of sculpture. I mean, that had to be tons of cantilevered marble.

Her carved face was intelligent. Predatory. A woman who took no crap from anyone. A woman who would always be about three jumps ahead. A woman who looked deeply into your eyes and would see the things you wanted to hide.

And then, with an electric shock, I saw the model for the statue. A woman. A large woman, but not much more than WNBA size. Yet she was unmistakably the real, live incarnation of the statue, down to the shield and the spear, though her spear was held at her side.

"Who is that, and would she like to spank me?" Christopher whispered.

"It's Athena," I said.

The name was out of my mouth before I even realized I knew the answer. And how did I know the answer? I don't know. Some buried memory of childhood. Some data bit gleaned from some long-forgotten DK mythology book.

"Athena," Jalil said, nodding like he naturally believed I knew.

Athena watched us. Said nothing. Gave no sign. Simply watched us pass.

I had felt as small as a bug. Now as I felt her gaze on my back I felt I wouldn't mind being even smaller.

Athena. Goddess of wisdom. Goddess of war.

What kind of society would join those two attributes in one goddess?

IV

It took something like two hours of walking to the accompaniment of the really annoying band before we reached the bottom stairs of Zeus's home or temple or whatever.

It was another fifteen minutes before we made it to the top. By which time we were sick of being awed and starting to get really annoyed. We were four kids in search of a toilet.

We were all breathing heavily by the last stair. The results of a very heavy breakfast. I made a mental note to control myself at the next meal. Then I made a mental note to forget that mental note: If I knew one thing for sure about Everworld it was that we'd inevitably end up hungry again.

To Zeus's credit, he knew how to welcome you to his home. Not him personally, of course, but some especially attractive servants who drew us into a side room and offered us washing water, something to drink, and a quick munchie. And a discreet curtained area to do what we each needed to do.

"We're the Beverly Hillbillies visiting the White House," Christopher commented.

"We're here to try and help the guy," David said, reassuring himself. "And at least he doesn't eat human hearts."

"Yeah. There's a solid character reference for you," Jalil said. "Have to set the bar kind of low in judging gods, huh?"

"Come this way," a servant said. "The Great One awaits."

Christopher raised his eyebrow. "The Great One? Jackie Gleason's here?"

"Who?" I asked.

"Jackie Gleason. You know, Ralph Kramden? *The Honeymooners*? That was his nickname: the Great One."

I said, "When cable goes out and you lose Nick at Nite, what do you do with yourself, Christopher?"

We'd done the Great Big Impressive Throne Room thing with Loki. And we'd been scared to death at that point. So the sight that met my eyes wasn't as overwhelming as it could have been.

Nevertheless, it was stunning. For one thing, Zeus seemed to have the first retractable dome roof in Everworld. The temple, or whatever it was, wasn't so much an enclosed space as an open theater. The spaces and distances were vast. But despite the rectangular exterior shape of the building, the interior, at least this monstrous room, was more of an oval.

The walls were stories of columns forming open galleries all around. The rows of columns changed with each story. Lower ones were simple fluted pillars. Higher up the pillars were mostly statues. Gods and goddesses, I suppose. So that the effect was of being a very tiny bug in the middle of a bright, exposed stage, surrounded by thousands and thousands of dour spectators, only some of whom seemed to think they should be clothed.

In addition to the open roof, the far end of the oval was open as well. Blue sky formed a sort of L, a bar across the sky, a bar vertically.

Not quite in the middle of the oval, closer to the open end, there was a platform. Not especially high, just a few steps, quite normal, human-sized steps.

On the platform, with plenty of room, stood two- or three-dozen gods, while below them, or darting in between them, there were maybe a hundred servants carrying drinks or platters of food. Other servants looked like the kind of crew that surrounds any movie star: hair people, wardrobe people, makeup people, gophers, and toadies.

You could almost guess who or what some of the gods were by who attended them. A slim, athletic young woman lounged back on a sort of uncomfortable easy chair. She reminded me of Mia Hamm. A nymph stood behind her, carrying a bow. Another held a quiver of arrows. Two young women fed delicacies to a trio of oversized greyhounds.

The gods and their servants ignored us as we approached. In fact, they seemed to be having a heated discussion — in between lounging and drinking. There was a press of big, beautiful bodies toward the center of the platform. With a few loungers, like the goddess with the bow, sitting a little apart or standing in smaller groups of two or three.

There was a definite sense that a particular individual was at the center of this debating society, but we couldn't see him. A servant noticed us and dove into the gods, worming his way between a loud, shrewish goddess and a sullen, angry-looking brute who glared at her from beneath brows that would have made a Neanderthal proud. I saw with a shock that he carried a sword, unsheathed. Blood dripped from the blade. Drop. Drop. Slowly. But the marble was never stained, no pool of blood appeared.

Suddenly from the crowd of gods staggered our old friend Dionysus. Dionysus seemed pretty normal in this assembly. He looked as he'd always looked to us, like a human guy, middle-aged and looking older from a lifetime of the worst kind of habits.

"Ah, my good fellows," he called to us.

"Dude," Christopher said and waved.

"You must take care till Zeus has changed his shape," Dionysus said. "No mortal can look upon Zeus's mighty countenance without dying. As my own poor mother, Semele, showed only too gruesomely."

"You have a mortal mother?" I asked.

"You're only half god, then, like Heracles," Jalil said.

Dionysus frowned and looked as if he might, if sober, have taken offense. "Half god? Nonsense. I was not born of a mortal woman, merely conceived. When Hera tricked my mother into asking Zeus to appear to her in his true form, my mother, naturally, shriveled and burned to a crisp till nothing was left but dust. I only survived because Zeus, my father, took me from Semele's womb and sewed me up inside his thigh till I could be born."

None of us had anything to say to that bizarre revelation.

"Okay," David said at last.

"So, since I was born of Zeus's thigh, clearly I am a god." He smiled a little smugly and drained his glass.

"You know, though," I said, eyeing the assembled gods, "you look . . . different. I mean, no offense, but you look older, smaller, you know, more normal than most of them."

Dionysus wasn't offended. He laughed. And suddenly in his place stood a laughing, handsome young man, the inevitable seven feet tall. "I look as people expect me to look," he said. "What is a god of wine and happy debauchery to look like?"

He reverted to his more relaxed style. He winked. "There is an element of entertainment, of theater, in this business of being a god, you know. Look at Artemis, lounging there with her hounds. She looks as the goddess of the hunt and protectress of virginity must look."

"Actually, she's not bad-looking, in a scary, Steffi Graf sort of way," Christopher said.

"Exactly," Dionysus said. "What on earth would be the point in a protectress of virgins who looked like Medusa? One must be wanted before refusal means anything. There's no virtue in an old hag remaining a virgin, after all." The glass of wine in his hand refilled itself and he took a long swig. He looked dubiously at me. "She'll like you, I suppose. And you as well," he added, looking at Jalil.

It was probably the first time I'd ever seen Jalil flustered. "Why would she like me?" he snapped.

Christopher snickered. David looked annoyed.

"Dionysus, what's going on here? Why are we supposed to be here?"

"Why? Do you not know that Olympus is besieged? Do you not know that the Hetwan are present in the thousands and tens of thousands? They are the greatest army assembled in one place since Agamemnon besieged Priam at Troy."

"Uh-huh. And we'd like to help, but what are we supposed to do about that?"

Dionysus winked. "I recall my pledge to grant you immortality. The matter of Christopher is quite easily arranged, since it was to him that I made the first vow. But the rest of you . . . well, I was concerned that the Great One might think I had overdone it. So first I had to gain you an audience with Himself. Thus, I told him that you were mighty warriors who had fought and defeated the Hetwan."

"You told him what?" David asked a bit shrilly.

"Yes. I have told Great Zeus that you can give

him victory over the Hetwan and that foul beast Ka Anor. And you can, you can, my boy. Surely it is time for a drink?"

"And yet," a new voice said, "to look at, none of you is a Hector or Achilles."

I turned, and there she was. The goddess from the statue. Serious but not grim. Skeptical but not hostile. I instinctively liked her. I hoped she wouldn't change my opinion. By squashing me like a bug.

A huge, ground-rumbling voice said, "Ah, Athena, my daughter. Now we can begin!"

Athena raised her gaze to look past us. She smiled, a smile of honest pleasure. "Yes, Father, I am here."

CHAPTER V

The crowd parted. Some with good grace, some welcoming, some grudging. A path opened. All but Ares, who stood his ground, dripping sword apparently never running out of blood.

And there, in view at last, Zeus.

Or at least a really big eagle. Not a bald eagle, not any kind of eagle I would recognize. This bird was sleek, black and gray with a bright yellow beak and yellow talons. He could also have swooped down and flown away with a UPS truck.

But he wasn't big on the scale of Nidhoggr. I was getting to be an expert on oversized things. This was a very, very large eagle. But not Nidhoggr size.

"Come to me, daughter," the eagle version of Zeus said.

Athena strode forward, her pace quickening.

She dropped to one knee before the eagle. "Father," she said.

"I find that my anger toward you has cooled, daughter," Zeus said. His beak moved as he spoke. Like it could actually create those ground-pounder bass notes.

Athena stood up. "Yes, I suspected that following the defeat of Ares's forces you might reconsider your anger at me."

The eagle face showed no reaction to this rather sarcastic reply. Ares's face grew even more simian. I got a feeling off Ares. A feeling that I didn't want to be alone in a room with him. He had the look of a hardened killer.

"Who are these mortals?" Zeus asked.

Every face turned toward us. How many gods? A lot. Some hard glares, some indifferent glances, resentful stares, and some coldly analytical appraisal.

"Dionysus has brought them," Athena said. "So I assume that they are fools, drunkards, and debauchers."

The eagle considered us. The eyes were like lasers. Maybe that's just what it's like to be stared at by an eagle. But I also sensed a deeper intelligence behind the gaze. I had the feeling that maybe Zeus was not a fool. And I was certain that Athena was not.

"These are the warriors you promised, Diony-sus?" Zeus asked skeptically.

"They do not look like much," Dionysus ad-mitted, "but they are great killers of Hetwan. This one —" He put his arm around David. "This one slew at least two dozen."

An exaggeration, but not by so much.

"Even this maiden has killed mighty Hetwan warriors."

The quality of the stares did not change. Ares spoke up. "I have warriors who have slain a hun-dred Hetwan. I have the sons of Ajax, of Hector, of Achilles himself. Many valiant warriors have slain Hetwan."

"I alone have slain more than a thousand," said a voice from behind a phalanx of gods. A man pushed his way through. He was built like a troll. He was thick in every limb, thick in his muscular torso, in his neck. He wore a sort of summer dress, belted with something that would have warmed the heart of a Texan truck driver. The dress unfortunately showed off two Austin Powers' movies' worth of chest hair.

"Damn, the Bears could use this guy on their offensive line," Christopher whispered.

Ares rolled his eyes. "Yes, yes, mighty Heracles has slain a great many Hetwan. But my mortals have slain more! We have made great piles of their bodies."

Heracles? *Hercules?* He looked nothing like Kevin Sorbo.

"And yet," Athena said, "the Hetwan now besiege Olympus itself. They surround us on three sides and will soon cut us off entirely. We replay the Trojan War, Father, and we are in the roles of the Trojans."

The eagle raised a hand — yes, a hand — gently silencing her. The talons were softening into legs. And a hand had appeared amid the feathers of one vast wing. Zeus was easing back to his own form.

"Who are you, mortals? Explain yourselves, and quickly." Suddenly a second hand appeared. And in that hand a bolt of lightning. It wasn't some cartoon lightning. It crackled and jerked, like true lightning. I felt my hair frizz from the static electricity. I felt the heat of it on my face. It was a twenty-foot-long, crooked, jumping, sizzling spear of lightning.

The four of us swallowed hard, all at once. I was pretty sure it wasn't my job to answer for us. David nodded slightly, as if agreeing to our unspoken plea that he act as spokesman.

Dionysus edged closer and whispered, "Speak up, be bold. He doesn't ask twice."

"We are from the old world," David said.

The eagle raised an eyebrow. "How have you come to be among us?"

David hesitated.

"Just tell him the truth, man," Jalil hissed. "You try to cover for Senna, he's going to thunderbolt our asses."

"We were carried here against our will when Loki . . ." David stopped. "Do you know Loki?"

"He is a minor god of the northern barbarians," Zeus said dismissively. His face was just beginning to appear, like a shadow on the face of the eagle.

"Okay. Well, he used his son, Fenrir, to snatch a girl named Senna. Senna was . . . is . . . a friend of ours."

Athena interrupted. "Why would Loki the trickster seize a girl of the real world?"

"She's a, uh, a witch," David said and stared hard at the floor. He looked like a man who has just committed treason and been caught at it. David had turned against Senna, at least to some extent. But he was still in her power. Even here, even now, many days from her last appearance.

I decided to speak. I said, "Look, she's supposed to be a witch. And Loki thinks she's some kind of gateway to the real world. Loki wants to use Senna to open a passage to the real world and escape there. Escape from Ka Anor."

"There have been rumors," a young god with little wings on his ankles and helmet said.

Zeus had become almost half human. He was an intriguing mix of eagle and man. I found I had a hard time looking at him. Like staring at the sun. I could look, but then I'd have to look away, eyes watering. The lightning didn't help. It snapped loudly and made me jump.

Athena took over the questioning. "So Loki has this witch?"

"No," I said. "Loki lost her. We've seen her since then, several times. She was involved with Huitzilopoctli. Merlin is chasing her, to keep her from being used as this gateway. And Ka Anor wants her, too."

"We know the wizard, Merlin," Athena said. "His wisdom runs deep." Before I could reply, she pressed on. "You passed through Ka Anor's city. What did you see?"

"We saw Ganymede eaten," Christopher blurted out.

A chill. A frisson, as they say. A sense that someone has said the unsayable. A disturbance in the role-playing of the gods of Olympus. Actual fear: not a common feeling here, I guessed.

But Athena was unmoved. "We shall miss Ganymede. But what did you see of the Hetwans' forces?"

Jalil answered. "They number tens of thousands. It's impossible to estimate more than that. But I think the real problem is that the Hetwan reproduce quickly. We learned from Ganymede that a single mating, while it costs the female her life, can produce eight or ten offspring. And I noticed that we saw no juvenile Hetwan, which leads me to suspect that Hetwan mature very quickly."

"They're easy to kill," David volunteered. "One-on-one, I mean. They have these weapons they use to shoot a kind of burning venom. But one-on-one, they can be taken." He nodded toward Ares and Heracles. "I don't doubt you can kill a lot of Hetwan. But can you stop them? That's a different question."

"It's a question of mathematics," Jalil said a little pedantically. "If we assume that they can put fifty thousand Hetwan in the field, and each can reproduce himself ten times over, then you have to kill them at a rate faster than they can reproduce. That's pretty unlikely."

"We will kill all who come against us!" Ares roared. "I will soak the fields with their blood!"

"I have slain a thousand. I will slay ten thousand," Heracles chimed in, equally enthusiastic. "Again and again we have charged into them. Again and again we have beaten back their assaults."

"The question is not how many Hetwan do you kill," Jalil said calmly. "But in what ratio? If you kill them one for one, you lose. If you kill them even two for one, or five for one, you lose. How many of your people have died against how many of theirs?"

"Many brave men lie dead in the fields," a tall, handsome, and somehow soulful god said with quiet authority.

"Apollo," Dionysus said in a stage whisper.

"The courage of our warriors undoes us," Apollo said. "Ares and Heracles lead them in bold charge after bold charge. But each time fewer come stumbling back. And now there are uncounted thousands of Hetwan. And no more than a thousand warriors on our side."

"What?" Christopher yelped. "They got you, what, fifty to one? Oh, man. I thought we could chill here. Freaking Ka Anor is going to be barbecuing your asses inside of a week!"

"I do not fear Ka Anor!" Ares said.

"Yeah? Well, I saw him eat your boy Ganymede. Let me tell you something, tough guy, if you're not afraid of Ka Anor you're even dumber than you look."

VI

I could literally watch the blood in Christopher's veins turn to ice. He had just dissed a god who looked like he pulled people's arms off for fun.

"I meant . . ." he said weakly.

Ares showed a lot of teeth from behind his black beard. "Good. My sword needs fresh meat." He moved toward Christopher. David started to draw his own sword, but suddenly Athena was there, putting her hand on his arm.

Dionysus, bless him, stepped forward, smiling at Zeus. "This mortal saved my life, Father. I promised him immortality in return."

Zeus now looked like a dignified older man. Kind of like Sean Connery with more hair and a gray Ulysses S. Grant beard. But there was a light inside him. As if beneath the skin were molten steel. As if touching him might crisp your finger. I could still only look at him for a few seconds before I felt uncomfortably warm and began to writhe in discomfort.

Zeus laughed. "Oh, Dionysus. Last time you offered immortality it was to that maiden, the blond. The one who inherited some special vineyard."

Dionysus spread his hands. "She was beautiful, she was willing, and she owns some of the finest grapes ever to grace a vine. That face! That body! That wine!"

There was a bit of a laugh from the gods. Then Zeus laughed and the laughter spread. Ares realized his killing spree had been called off. So did Christopher and he nearly swooned.

"If immortality you have vowed, then immortality he shall have," Zeus said. "We rejoice that you escaped Ka Anor, Dionysus. What would our revels be without you? Step forward, mortal."

Christopher took one step forward. Thought about it and took two more. "Um, no thanks," he said and stepped back.

Zeus blinked. "You refuse immortality?"

"Yeah. I mean, yes, sir. Your . . . your godhood."

"No one refuses immortality," Zeus said. "Do they?"

"No," came a chorus of disgruntled voices.

"It's not that I don't think it's cool," Christopher

said. "It's just that I don't deserve it. Ganymede saved my life. But when I might have saved him, I ran. So it's, like, this is in payment. It's kind of an honor thing."

Zeus looked blank. All the gods and all their servants looked blank.

David and Jalil looked amazed.

"Say *what*?" Jalil muttered.

"Look, it's no big thing. I pay what I owe people, all right? I didn't pay Ganymede. This is how I pay the price."

Only Apollo showed any comprehension. "You feel you owe a debt."

"Yeah. Yes. Sir."

"Yes, well, it's a very stupid thing to do," Apollo said.

"Well," Zeus said, clearly nonplussed. "Now what?"

"We've been insulted!" Ares bellowed. "Cast this mortal down. Let him fall for a week and then let him be plunged into the depths of the sea!"

"Oh, shut up, Ares," Artemis muttered.

Ares lunged toward her, sword raised. I recoiled instinctively. Artemis was on her feet, an arrow in her bow, string drawn back to her ear in less time than it took me to flinch.

The two gods glared at each other. Bloody sword and graceful bow ready, quivering.

The attractive older goddess who I later learned was Hera began yelling, mostly at Artemis, as though it were her fault. Apollo, for no apparent reason, was berating Dionysus. In a flash two-dozen gods were yelling, screaming, roaring, and threatening. The sound shook the marble floor. Dark clouds boiled into view, covering the sun.

It was as if someone had thrown a switch. In a few seconds the immortals had become crazed, raving lunatics. Lunatics with the power to alter reality around them through the sheer force of emotion. A whirlwind was forming, a tornado that swirled around the stage. Thunder boomed. Electricity crackled. At least three of the gods stormed away, slamming brutally through unwary servants who scattered before them or were crushed underfoot.

I covered my ears with both hands. I was standing inside a thunderstorm. The wind tore at my clothes, whipped my hair into my face, stinging my eyes. The force of it nearly knocked me down. I was one of those newspeople standing out in the hurricane holding onto a streetlamp and shouting, "The winds are really powerful, Dan!"

Madness. One minute they were talking, lounging around like it was an unhappy family reunion, the next minute they were snarling dogs.

Only Athena stood apart, watching, her lip

curled in contempt. She stood in a pocket of calm. No wind touched her. I almost believed that no crash of thunder or bellow reached her.

"We need to back slowly out of this room," David said, yelling to be heard over the uproar and the wind. "These guys are nuts. Slowly. Don't turn away from them."

I agreed. These creatures were insane. These creatures were dangerous. We began to back away, holding on to one another to keep from being blown down.

"Hold!" Zeus said in his crack-the-walls voice.

The bickering and shouting didn't stop. But we did.

"I can't move," Jalil said. He shot me a desperate look. I couldn't move, either. My feet had been Krazy-Glued to the floor. I could writhe, I could lean and struggle, but I could not move my feet.

Zeus stood, towering over the other gods, and he was growing larger still. He was fully humanoid now. I guess that's the word. He looked like a human. Sean Connery with a beard. A very angry Sean Connery with massive thunderbolts crackling and snapping in his fist.

He took a step forward, kicked Dionysus with one gold-sandaled foot, and sent our most familiar god tumbling and skidding across the floor.

Then he reached down one garage-door-sized hand and yanked Ares up by his heels. Ares kicked impotently, his head swinging just a foot off the floor.

Zeus threw the god of war. Threw him tumbling through the air till he slammed backward into a third-story pillar that seemed to be a likeness of Hera.

Ares fell to the floor. Took a few seconds, like an injured football player, then stood up, obviously winded.

"Ares is angry!" Ares yelled between gasps for breath.

"Zeus is angry!" Zeus thundered, playing his own name like a trump card. He drew back a crackling lightning bolt, ready to launch it.

"I will fight no more for Olympus!" Ares cried, sounding a lot like a big, very dangerous five-year-old. He stormed — literally — from the room, pushing his way through two pillars and cracking each in the process.

Now the bickering settled down a little. One by one the gods, many red in the face from rage, quieted. The storm was gone.

I was shaken. Alarmed. I let go of Christopher's hand, pushed my hair back into place, and untwisted my dress.

"Here's an idea," Christopher whispered. "No one say anything to piss them off."

"We've lost Ares," Heracles said gloomily.

"We've lost little enough, then," Athena said dismissively.

A reduced number of gods settled back into chairs or standing poses. The whirlwind had dissipated. The thunder was silent. The sky above cleared.

"And they wonder why they're getting their butts kicked by the Hetwan," David said under his breath.

But not so quietly that Athena failed to hear. "What did you say, mortal?"

"David, remember me saying, 'Don't piss them off again'?" Christopher moaned.

"Yeah. You know what? Screw their little temper tantrums. I'm tired of this. This is what comes from having your butt kissed for thousands of years. Reality time for the gods starts right now."

I think all three of us were proud of David at that moment.

And all three of us edged slowly away from him.

CHAPTER VII

"Great, you're going to set them off again," Christopher said.

But David stepped forward. He was mad. I could tell. He wasn't even trying to hide it. Not from us or from them.

Truth was, our natural deference toward any seven-foot immortal was beginning to fray. We were all getting sick of the gods.

"I said, it's no surprise the Hetwan are beating you," David said.

A faint hint of a smile on Athena's face.

"He mocks the gods!" the guy with the wings on his ankles said.

Athena calmly lowered her spear and pressed the point against the winged god's chest. "Silence, Hermes. As long as he speaks the truth, he is under my protection." To David she said, "Continue."

David tried to hook his thumbs in his back pockets, then realized he didn't have any pockets. "Look, the Hetwan are united. One god. One boss. And all the males are basically soldier-priests. Totally loyal. Absolutely fearless. Ka Anor says die, they die. Ka Anor says kill, they kill. And Ka Anor doesn't argue with Ka Anor."

Athena nodded in satisfaction. "A mortal can see it!" she cried. "A fool of a mortal from the old world can see what the gods of Olympus cannot. We cannot fight a united foe when we are not united."

"And all must be united under Athena, of course," Hera said poisonously. "We must all bend our knee to Athena."

"This is not the Trojan War," Athena argued. "Nor is it any of the great wars we've seen since the birth of Everworld. We have always taken whatever side pleased us, choosing this mortal or that to favor. We contended against one another using mortals as our pawns. And —"

"Thus it has always been," Apollo said, mildly critical. "How else are mortals to know our power? How else are mortals to learn that we are watching over them?"

"This is different," Athena said. "This is not a war of man against man. This is like the ancient wars when Mighty Zeus led all the race of gods to defeat the Titans and gain mastery of the world. Once more we must unite, put aside all jealousies, all pettiness, bring all our powers to bear, and —"

"And simply obey you," a languid feminine voice said.

She was a goddess I hadn't seen before. I realized it was because she'd been lying on a sort of couch behind the crowd.

Now she did a slow catwalk strut toward us. She wore an almost entirely transparent dress that clung to every last curve of her Playmate of the Year body. She was the female equivalent of Ganymede: impossibly beautiful. So beautiful she moved even women, even me. So beautiful that she made Athena and Hera, both of whom were lovely, look like lunchroom ladies.

Just behind her and slightly above, there flew a slim young man. He might have been as young as fourteen. He might have been as old as sixteen. Of course in reality he was centuries old. But his appearance was of a slim, feminine teen built to about half of normal size. He slowly flapped a pair of angel's wings and held a small bow. Beside the lush goddess he seemed like a cherub.

"Who else should direct the war?" Athena demanded. "You, Aphrodite?"

I glanced at my friends. If it were up to them Aphrodite could be queen of the world. I've never seen three more idiotic, sappy expressions. Jalil was unconsciously straightening his clothes. David's righteous anger had burned out to be replaced by a half smile, a gulping throat, and eyes that seemed to be preparing him for an SAT-length test on Aphrodite's physical description.

Christopher actually gave a limp little wave and said, "Hi."

"Ares is the god of war," Aphrodite said in her come-to-me voice. "He leads our warriors. And he . . ." she said, running her tongue slowly over her lips and causing David to groan, ". . . is a fabulous lover."

The flying boy-god giggled and made an obscene motion. Then he winked at me.

"Go to him, then, Aphrodite," Athena said disgustedly. "Go to Ares, and take your pigeon with you."

"Pigeon?" the flying boy echoed mockingly. "I am wounded. What a surprise that the virgin goddess of wisdom has no love for Eros."

"She knows nothing of love," Aphrodite said pityingly to Eros. "She loves men only as babbling philosophers or deadly warriors. How strange that she should love both the tongue and the sword . . ." She paused for effect, like Mae West vamping. ". . . And yet she partakes of neither the tongue nor the sword."

That brought a raucous laugh from Eros and a snicker from Hermes.

Aphrodite, having delivered her line, and having caused David, Jalil, and Christopher to entirely forget where they were, what they were doing, or, indeed, their own names, sauntered away like the one happy supermodel on the catwalk.

Zeus looked depressed. Athena followed Aphrodite with her angry eyes. So did Artemis, but with a certain vague appreciation.

"What are we to do?" Zeus asked plaintively.

With the goddess of love gone David snapped back to a semblance of reality. But only a semblance. "Show us the defenses," he said, glancing after Aphrodite. "Show us the . . . the, um, battlefield."

That brought Christopher back to reality. "What?"

"Look, these guys are hopeless," David said, making no attempt to whisper. "Look at them. Ka Anor is coming, they've got Hetwan crawling all over their land, and they still can't get their act together. They can't form a democracy; they can't form a dictatorship. It's like trying to get a room full of cats to cooperate."

Exactly, I thought. Like cats. They weren't being deliberately stupid, they were acting according to their natures. They were what they were. Very powerful two-year-olds.

"It's the way they all are," I said without thinking. "All the gods. Loki and Hel and Huitzilopoctli and now these guys." I looked at Athena. "You can't do it, can you? It's your weakness. You can't change? I mean, you literally can't change. Dionysus will always be a drunk, and Aphrodite will always be a slut, and Ares will always be bloodthirsty. Always. No matter what."

Athena flared angrily and I thought I'd overdone it. She'd told David to tell the truth, not me. But her anger was only a passing shadow. Behind it came sadness. "The doom of the gods," she said softly. "We are as we are. It is mortal man who changes."

David said, "Look, you have to win this fight. Period. You gods of Olympus are some of the greatest powers of Everworld. I mean, that's what we hear, anyway. You're the most numerous, the most organized. You have this mountain, which works for you. If you lose to Ka Anor, who's going to stop him?"

"We will never lose!" Heracles cried, literally thumping his chest. "Our warriors are the most valiant of mortals. And Great Zeus the most powerful of gods."

For the first time Jalil spoke up. Not angry like

David, not disgusted like me. Calm. Reasonable. Almost indifferent. "It doesn't matter how brave you are. The Hetwan don't care how brave you are. In fact, if your bravery leads you to do stupid things then the Hetwan are glad you're brave. This isn't Troy. This isn't one guy with a sword against another guy with a sword. If you're going to beat them you need to be smarter than they are."

Athena nodded. "I know this. And yet . . ." Her gaze flickered, uncertain. "I have always been the protector of warriors who were both wise and bold: Perseus when he slew Medusa, Bellerophon, Jason, Diomedes, and of course, the great and incomparable Odysseus, who defeated Troy not with brutish force, but with guile."

The name Odysseus made her smile, a wistful, faraway look. And for a moment she was lost in memory. "But no Odysseus has shown himself in our armies. No Jason or Perseus. Who will be my great warrior? Who will be wise in war? Who will turn the tide of battle against the Hetwan?" She raised her hand and pointed a finger at David. "You?"

There wasn't a doubt in my mind what David would say.

"Yes. Put me in charge. Us," he amended, with a nod at the rest of us. "Put us in charge. We'll beat the Hetwan for you."

CHAPTER
VIII

"So now you're Odysseus?"

We were walking behind Athena, heading away from Zeus and the rest of the mad menagerie of immortals. The four of us, looking like the dork squad behind the big, powerful, and beautiful goddess of wisdom and war.

Christopher had the nerve to tease David, but even he didn't have the nerve to check out Athena.

I was getting to be an expert on immortals. As expert as anyone has been in a long, long time, anyway. I was starting to draw some conclusions. They were always touchy. They were always strange. Difficult. Rigid and inflexible. Immoral.

Or maybe amoral is the right word, although what's the real difference between having no morals and having bad morals? In the end it leaves you doing whatever you want.

I wondered if the gods were a species. Like humans or apes or David's example, house cats. They looked human for the most part. Bigger. More powerful. Sometimes they glowed with an unnatural light. They seemed able to change their looks, to morph into different creatures, to get bigger or smaller.

But maybe all of that was illusion. Were they just humans with some magical abilities, or were they, despite outward appearances, as different from us as we are from gorillas?

Were they built from the twisted molecule of DNA just like any animal? Were they, after all, just humans plus or minus a few chromosomes?

I wished I could talk to Jalil about it. No doubt he had a theory. In fact I could see the carefully blank expression he wears whenever he thinks he's figured something out.

One thing was sure: I had not met a god like Athena before. She was no Hel, no Huitzilopoctli, no Loki, or even Dionysus. She was, after all, a goddess of wisdom. Maybe that really counted for something. She was the closest I'd seen to a sane god. And yet, even she admitted she could not change.

She led the way along an endless corridor. At

the far end, a perfect rectangle of blue sky. She said nothing as we walked, and out of awe or fear or simple prudence, we didn't say anything, either.

Aside from Christopher's stage whispers.

"Shouldn't it be Davideus," he suggested. "I mean, Odysseus, Perseus, and who else?"

"Diomedes," Jalil supplied. "But also Bellerophon and Jason."

"Davideus," Christopher said, undeterred. "Davideus Levineus. The first J —, um, the first, um . . . American Greek hero."

He'd been on the edge of saying the first Jewish Greek hero. He'd stopped himself. He had stopped himself and then collapsed into babble and unfunniness.

"You know, I'm trying," he muttered. "But politically correct isn't funny."

David said, "Christopher, it wouldn't bother me you saying I was the first Jewish Greek hero. That's cool. Of course I'm only half Jewish, but that's okay just the same."

"Well, Jesus, how am I supposed to know what's cool and what's not?" Christopher exploded.

Jalil said, "How about a rationing system? You get zero the words that really make us want to kick your ass but you can have one 'Hebrew' and one 'brutha,' each pronounced with suitable derision, per day. On special occasions you get a bonus 'brutha.'"

That made us all laugh, and Athena turned to look over her shoulder at us like a stern teacher escorting the class clowns to the principal's office.

But she didn't try to kill us. Which set her apart from the general run of gods.

We stepped out through the rectangle of sky and I felt the wind sucked out of me. We were at the edge of nothingness. We were above the clouds. Like being in a plane.

I was looking down at the clouds, and down through the breaks in the clouds at picture-postcard fields, at vineyards, at silver streams and whitewashed villages.

And over it all, a wash of brown. It was as if there'd been a flood of sewage or something. The brown tide filled the roads, stained the fields, surged between the homes and farms.

The Hetwan were everywhere. They washed right up against the sheer sides of Olympus itself.

Athena stood there, robes blowing in the stiff, warm breeze, and tilted her helmeted head back. "Come to me, Bellerophon's steed. Come to me, Pegasus, and bring your brood!"

"Did she say Pegasus?" Christopher asked.

I grabbed his arm and pointed upward. At first it might have been a flock of seagulls, white against blue. But the illusion that they were birds disappeared as they neared. They were horses, all right. White horses with great big feathered white wings.

"Well, I know I should be tired of saying this by now, but that is just impossible," Jalil said, sounding disgusted. "You cannot lift a horse into the air with bird wings. And how does it turn? It has a horse tail not feathers. It couldn't turn. But it does."

"W.T.E.," David said.

"Yes, Welcome To Everworld, I know," Jalil grumbled.

Four flying horses swooped down toward us, hooves tucked up, tails flapping idly with the wind, heads held high without regard to aerodynamics, wings slowly beating.

Had I ever seen anything more beautiful? Had I ever in my life, here in Everworld, or my real life back in the world, had I ever seen anything to compare? It made me want to cry for a universe where no such creature existed or could exist.

I could see myself walking across the quad talking to friends and looking up to see . . . I could picture myself gazing out of a window at home, at school, and seeing . . .

Nostrils black, hooves black, eyes a brown so dark it was black, details that defined a whiteness so intense, so luminous it could not be natural.

The largest of the horses slowed his momentum just like any bird, by flaring his wings. Magnificent. What other word could apply? Magnificent.

He landed nimbly beside us, hooves clattering, easily shedding the rest of his speed.

"When Athena calls, Pegasus comes," the horse said.

"It talks," Jalil said. "And I'm not even surprised."

The other three horses circled slowly overhead. A merry-go-round in the sky.

Athena patted the horse's neck affectionately. "I have need of you and your sons, Pegasus. I beg you to carry this mortal and to instruct your sons to carry his companions. Take them where they will. Show them the armies gathered below. Bear them and do their bidding, for love of Athena."

Pegasus nodded briskly, like a competent subordinate taking orders.

To David she said, "Go, ride with Pegasus and see all that may be seen of the armies below and their dispositions. Then consider how Olympus may be saved."

Athena didn't wait around for David to snap a salute. She disappeared. Literally. One second she was there, and then she wasn't. Her bulk had sheltered me a bit from the breeze, and suddenly it didn't.

"Well, Davideus Maximus, show us how it's done," Christopher said, ushering David toward the winged horse.

"Um, there's no saddle," David said, not sounding much like a mythical hero.

"No man saddles Pegasus," Pegasus said.

"Okay," David said. Then, in an aside to us, "I'm talking to a horse."

"Jump on board," Jalil suggested.

"Uh-huh. You jump on board. You some kind of horseman, Jalil?"

"Mmm, no. I'm definitely not. Which is why I'm waiting for you to show me how it's done."

David looked like he was getting his nerve up for a Lone Ranger leap when Pegasus simply lowered and extended one wing. David stepped gingerly on it. His sneaks left faint footprints on the Ivory Snow white of the feathers. But within seconds the marks were gone.

He walked precariously up the wing, then settled awkwardly into place.

"Okay," he said dubiously.

Pegasus stood, folded his wing back, turned, reared up like a TV horse, and leaped into emptiness.

David yelled. A very unheroic sound. I ran to the edge, half expecting to see the horse and David spiraling down to crash against the cliff.

But Pegasus spread his wings and caught the updraft. He swooped slowly, gracefully away. He flew. A horse. With a guy on his back.

"You'd think I'd be used to it by now," Jalil said. "I'm just not. Just for the record, let me repeat, that can't be happening."

One by one Pegasus's sons, all more or less identical to Pegasus, though a shade smaller, swooped down and carried away Christopher, Jalil, and finally me. Finally me because I wasn't excited about the idea.

Horses, fine. Flying horses were a different story. Amazing and heart-stoppingly beautiful they might be, but that didn't mean I wanted to ride one.

Still, there was no denying that David, Jalil, and Christopher all seemed to be okay. And a flying horse wasn't the most impossible thing I'd seen in Everworld. I had, after all, seen Nidhoggr fly.

Still, when my horse landed to pick me up I had to drag myself into place. It wasn't an easy thing to do. Unlike a normal horse where you can just let your legs dangle down, or else stick them in stirrups, on a winged horse you have to sit with your feet either pulled up and forward, or else pulled up and back in a kneeling position. Otherwise your legs hang right on the wings. And in addition to getting in the way of the wings' movements, it looks ridiculous with your legs rising and falling with each wing stroke. Jalil had been doing that for a while and he looked like a marionette.

So I made my way, wincing with each step, up the wing and I tucked my feet back into a semi-kneel, and the horse calmly ran off the edge of a cliff.

At which point I screamed.

Sheer unholy terror.

I had nothing to hold on to, nowhere to put my feet, and this wasn't a horse running across the meadow — this was a horse running in midair.

I was balanced on his back. I squeezed my knees to hold on but that was nothing to bet your life on. It was like riding on an airplane. Not in a plane, on a plane. Outside.

The horse moved in a way that felt like a long, liquid gallop. As though he were a Derby winner filmed in slow motion. Wings came up and threw my hair back off my face, wings came down and I would feel the back of the horse surge up against me.

"Don't let me fall," I said to the horse.

"I won't," he reassured me.

"What's your name?" I asked him, stopping just short of adding a patronizing "boy."

"Pelias. In honor of King Pelias."

"Ah. King Pelias. Of course. Just don't drop me, Pelias."

Pelias turned into a slow, descending arc, intersecting his father and brothers. Four horses with four extremely nervous riders came together in a loose V formation, with Pegasus out in front.

We matched speed with the breeze, which made it seem as if there were no breeze at all except the regular backwash from Pelias's wings.

"Anyone else scared?" I yelled.

"Oh, yeah," Christopher said.

We were in a dream. The kind of dream you think is charming and thrilling later, after you wake up. The four of us in a still, quiet zone, hanging there, as if we were all forms on a mobile above a baby's bed.

I could see forever. Olympus behind us blocked the view in that direction, but far off, and yet not far enough, I could see an emptiness in the trees, a blank circle that was the crater city of Ka Anor.

Then Pegasus led us downward, circling down like buzzards descending on roadkill. Down into the white cotton clouds that bathed my skin in moisture and blinded me to everything but myself.

The horse seemed to disappear, his color identical to the cloud. It took my breath away. I was riding an invisible horse, just a girl crouching in a too-formal dress, rising and falling with the rhythm of unseen wings in the middle of a blank nothingness.

Jalil appeared, emerged from the clouds, a vision that faded almost as soon as it appeared. Ahead I caught a glimpse of David, like me, like Jalil, a human figure flying, kneeling with legs spread wide by an unseen mount.

Then we fell below the clouds, out into clear air. My horse reappeared between my knees.

For a while longer as we flew, as we descended slowly, my head would plow upside-down furrows in the clouds. Then the clouds became a ceiling. And at last, mere clouds again.

Then we were in an open patch of blue between clouds, and Olympus loomed far above us. I couldn't see the shining city that hid on its tabletop, not from this angle below. No one on the ground below would ever be able to catch even a glimpse of Zeus's city.

The walls of Mount Olympus were mostly pretty sheer, absolute cliffs of gray rock in some places, some showing evidence of massive rock slides. But it was not all impassable. We had, after all, ascended to Olympus on foot and mule.

The mountain was part of, yet apart from, a mountain chain that extended to the left and right, maybe east to west, maybe north to south, I had no idea. I decided arbitrarily to think of it as north and south, with Olympus sticking out toward the west.

The mountain chain drew a rugged line, with Olympus thrust forward. One side of Olympus was connected with the mountain chain by means of a high, narrow ridge. The top of the ridge looked as if it could accommodate no more than ten men or women walking abreast. Both sides were sheer, rocky drops that looked as if they suffered a rock slide every day. The length of the ridge was like a suspension bridge, lower in the middle, higher at the ends where it met Olympus and the unnamed mountain beyond.

We had come to Olympus from the south-southwest, up a winding road that was lined at the lower altitudes with villages, shops and stalls and stables. That was presumably the easiest approach.

But we had traveled that road just the day before and had encountered no Hetwan blocking it. Even now the road seemed open and the villagers were unmolested. I saw an oxcart ascending slowly. I saw men at work in steep fields, walking behind plows drawn by mules. I saw women beating laundry against rocks beside an explosively fast mountain stream.

No Hetwan there. Why? Why not come right up that road?

Pelias followed Pegasus around the mountain and we came in view of the main area of battle. It was the western face of the mountain. That face was very rough, very sheer, but with several odd little plateaus, as if some unimaginably huge creature had cut steps in the mountainside.

I counted six of these step plateaus, ranging from a space about the size of a football field, up to the size of a mall parking lot. The slopes had only a sparse covering of gnarled trees, but these plateaus seemed to have been deliberately cultivated. There were trees in rows, presumably orchards of some sort. And there were grapevines. But also open, grassy spaces, and even small, crude huts or barns made of piled stones.

The Hetwan had evidently seized the lowest of the six platforms. And I could clearly see a network of wooden steps either finished or being constructed, that would carry their army rushing the three hundred feet up to the next plateau.

The Greeks, clearly visible in upper body armor that flashed in the sun, occupied that next plateau. Maybe there really were the thousand men that

Ares had claimed. But they didn't look that numerous.

They had pitched brightly colored tents crammed toward the back of the platform, back within an orchard of six or eight dozen trees. The whole plateau was perhaps two thousand feet long and half that wide at its widest point. Many were gathered around cooking fires, eating, drinking, and laughing loudly enough that the sound floated up to me in the sky, high above. If they were beaten men, they didn't seem to know it. I saw faces turned up to watch us pass by. Dark, olive-complected men with black hair and black eyes, some bearded, some clean-shaven.

We flew above and past the battlefield, heading around to view the north side of the mountain.

"Why don't they at least build some barricades or something?" Jalil asked.

"These guys fight with swords and spears," David said. "Hard to hack at someone when you have to reach over a barricade. They fight man-to-man, sword against . . . against Hetwan stingers, I guess."

"They have guys with bows and arrows," Christopher pointed out. "They could shield them at least."

"They could," David agreed. "You know, what

we're seeing here is war without the last two thousand years of experience and advancement."

"Is that what we've been doing with war? Advancing?" I asked. "Able to kill more people much faster?"

"Look at that," David complained as we pulled away. "They're letting the damned Hetwan build steps right up to the plateau. They could burn them out without too much effort. At least harass them, slow them down."

The north face of the mountain was rugged and cut deeply by a stream that sliced through rock and leaped in several spectacular falls.

"Okay, I guess we've seen what there is to see," David said.

But something had caught my eye. "Let's keep on for another minute," I called out to him.

We flew on around the north face of the mountain, and there it was: a canyon that descended from near the top of the mountain down to a point just lower than the leading Hetwan edge.

"Look at that," I yelled to the others as the horses turned a slow clockwise. "That canyon. Probably it was formed by that river, then changed course. Or else some other river that dried up. But look."

"I see it," David said, mystified. "So what?"

I was a little surprised. David couldn't see what

it meant? Maybe I was wrong. Or not. "You could move down that canyon, out of sight of the Hetwan. It could bring you down, parallel with the Hetwan army and they wouldn't even see it. You could bring the good guys across, up out of the canyon, travel down along that fold, and hit the Hetwan from the side. The problem is," I added, "they could do the reverse. They could come up that canyon, climb above the Greeks, and cut them off, trap them."

David swept into my view. He was flushed bright red. "Yeah," he said. "Yeah, that's true."

"Oh, my god," Christopher said, unwilling to let pass any opportunity to take a poke at David. "The general's been out-Napoleoned. By a chick."

But David, once he was past his momentary embarrassment, was gracious. "She has a good eye for terrain. She's right. You're right, April. If the Greeks had used that canyon when they had some numbers they could have cut off the advance force of Hetwan, chewed 'em up, and then bailed before the Hetwan brought up reinforcements."

I was pleased, though not for any good reason, I'm sure. I was talking about helping people kill one another. Still, it was cool. I had a "good eye for terrain."

But Pegasus had a better eye. "Battle is begun!"

he cried, and the four winged mounts beat wings back toward the western slope.

"We're not getting into this now, are we?" Christopher demanded.

"Looks like," Jalil said.

I said, "David. We're not just going to jump into this, are we? I mean, aren't we supposed to help with planning or whatever?"

He turned partly to grin a happy, cocky grin. "April, we're about a thousand years away from generals who lead from the rear. That would be one of those 'advancements' you were being sarcastic about."

"I take it back. Let's be advanced. Let's lead from the rear. Progress."

He laughed. "Next battle. Not this one. This one we get sweaty."

CHAPTER
X

Down we swept, like fighter planes, like we were going to come in Red Baron style and start shooting at the Hetwan on the ground.

Of course that wasn't happening. Instead we were just racing to join the embattled Greeks.

"Where are the gods?" I demanded. "Where are all the so-called gods? Why aren't they helping?"

These were just men below us, or so it seemed to me. I saw some big, strong, fabulously armored men wearing helmets with three-foot-long feathers, but none of the gods of Olympus. No Apollo. No Artemis with her bow. No Ares or Zeus. And no Athena.

The Hetwan had finished their spidery, interlaced network of ladders and platforms and steps. Easy to see why they'd built the structure: They were not designed by nature for walking uphill. They had wings. When they needed to move up a steep hill they could fly. Only they weren't flying.

They were swarming up, hundreds, maybe thousands, moving in disciplined rows, follow the leader and no shoving. Impossible not to think of ants.

The Hetwan charging outnumbered the Greek defenders four or five to one. But by no means was the whole Hetwan force involved. A far larger number milled far below, down on the first plateau. And more still spread through the surrounding countryside, seemingly indifferent.

We were no more than twenty feet in the air when the two ranks of fighters, Hetwan and Greek, slammed into each other with a roar of human voices and a crash of sword and shield.

We zoomed over before I could see much more than a blur. Pelias landed more smoothly than a commercial jet. One second he ran on air, the next his hooves thudded madly across grass and rock.

David leaped first from his horse and raced for the tents. He looked as if he was running away, trying to put as much distance as possible between himself and the battle.

"Come on, help me!" he cried over his shoulder.

Greek warriors were rushing past us, heading for battle, all grinning maniacally through their beards, buckling helmets into place, drawing swords, quaffing final gulps of wine.

We pushed through them, ignored, then we were alone among the tents, rushing, running, confused. All but David.

"Start tearing up these tents. Pull up the tent poles. Do it!"

It was as if he'd been assigned the job of breaking camp and was determined to do it in record time.

I glanced up and saw Pegasus and his children float by, clean and pure and safe above us, heading back for the altitude of the gods. Wished I was with them. I was in a dress, racing around a soldiers' camp, trying to work six-foot tent poles up out of the ground.

Jalil had Excalibur, his Swiss Army knife with the two-inch Coo-Hatch steel blade that would cut through anything. He was slicing the colored canvas tents into strips.

David grabbed the first long strip of canvas and wound it around my tent pole, tying the ends with the ease of a good amateur sailor.

"Here. Olive oil, I think," Christopher said, hauling a big pottery pitcher toward the closest campfire. Either David had told him what was expected or Christopher had figured it out on his own. "I don't know how well it'll burn."

David nodded and thrust the clothed end of the tent pole into the jar. Then he stuck the greasy wad into the fire.

It took a few seconds, but then the canvas began to burn, a black-smoke fire.

David grabbed his torch, shot me a grin that was no different from that of the Greek warriors. "Keep 'em coming," he yelled and took off, running like a pole jumper toward the clash of battle.

"Let's go for it," Jalil said calmly.

We began work on two more torches. It took less time now that we knew what we were doing. We had one ready in a minute. I grabbed it up.

"I'll take it up forward," Jalil said quickly.

"I can do this," I said. Not resentful. Just telling it true. I might not have the strength to do much damage in a sword fight, but I could do this.

I ran, balancing the burning pole on my shoulder, which was bruised and raw within twenty paces. The Greek fighters had their backs to me; they were pressed in tight, pushing to reach the Hetwan. There were swords and spears everywhere. It was like trying to push through a crowd of porcupines.

"Look out! Move it!" I yelled.

A young officer noticed me and began punching and pummeling his soldiers to get them to form a lane. I pushed through, into the mass of men. The sound of killing was a solid wall of noise, all around me. Men yelled, men cried out, men called on the gods, men threatened, men exulted in triumph.

Then, all at once, I was there, in the front. Greeks hacked with stunning violence at Hetwan who fired their Super Soakers. These weren't choreographed sword fights going on all around me. This wasn't Hollywood. These were madmen hacking and hacking with all their might, sinking blades deep into Hetwan flesh. Hetwan body parts were everywhere.

But the Hetwan were far from helpless. Greek warriors bellowed like enraged animals as the Hetwan venom caught fire and burned through armor and leather and flesh.

A warrior spun, clutching his face. A one-inch round of Hetwan fire burned inside his left eye socket, burned its way sizzling and popping through the eye while his right eye stared out in agony.

I saw David. Pushed toward him. Wanted to close my eyes to the violence all around me. A big man slammed against me, hands clutching, missing. He fell. No fire. I saw a neat, one-inch hole that passed through his helmet. There was only a slight trickle of blood dribbling down his sweaty forehead. He collapsed facedown, dead beyond question. An identical one-inch hole came out the back of his helmet. Only this hole was clogged with red-gray brain.

"April!" David yelled.

"Look at him," I cried.

"He's dead," David said harshly. "Give me the torch."

He took it from me. I registered the fact as if it were happening to someone else. A hole, right through the helmet twice and clear through the head. A bullet? Someone had guns? What else could it be?

I ran to stay with David. He had to see, he had to understand. Something was very wrong. He stood surrounded by half a dozen Greeks who had formed a sort of bodyguard to protect him as he pushed through the Hetwan. He took a good hold on the torch and launched it like a spear over the edge.

The Greeks had gotten the idea now. Jalil appeared with another torch and David launched it. I raced back to the camp, passing Christopher on the way.

"Is it working?" he gasped.

"I don't know."

How many times did I make that run? How many times did I wind canvas, and tie it off, and soak it with oil, and set it on fire, and go running back through the corridor the Greeks now kept open? I lost count. It seemed like a hundred times. Like all I'd ever done in my entire life was run back and forth carrying flaming, smoking torches.

I kept one eye at a time closed because the smoke and my own sweat stung. I'd laid a patch of canvas on my shoulder, a pitiful attempt to keep the bouncing torch poles from lacerating me any further.

But still the Hetwan advanced and the Greeks, inch by inch, bleeding for every inch, fell back.

"You can stop. Can't reach the edge anymore, can't get within range to throw," David said to me at last. He had come back through the Greek line and practically collapsed as he swilled water from a jar held by a servant.

"It didn't work?" I asked.

"Yeah, it worked fine," he said. "All the Hetwan steps are burning. They can't bring up fresh troops. We just have to stop these guys. We'll get them."

"David, they have some kind of weapon. Like a gun or something."

"What?"

"I saw a guy with a hole that went all the way

through his head. Through the helmet. I've never seen a bullet hole, but that was a bullet hole."

"They're fighting with their Super Soakers," he said, dubious. "Why would they do that if they had guns? And besides, I didn't hear a gunshot."

"I did," Jalil said. He'd come panting and wheezing up with another torch. "Didn't know what it was. It sounded like a loud bang. Just once."

David forced a laugh. "Let's hope you're both wrong. If they have guns, we're dead. Damn!"

I followed the direction of his gaze. Two or three dozen Hetwan had taken wing and were flying around to our right, trying to join the ranks of their depleted forces.

"Archers!" David yelled at the top of his lungs. "Archers to the right flank."

Half a dozen Greeks went racing by, pulling arrows from their quivers and slotting them on the run.

Arrows flew and the Hetwan fell. So that was why the Hetwan didn't fly into battle. They were too big, too slow. They were impossible to miss for a trained bowman.

A warrior, maybe twice David's size, came rushing up. He was armored, sweating. There was blood in his black beard. "Our men tire, Davideus."

I registered the "Davideus" that had been a

joke to Christopher. The man pronounced it with a flat "a." Like avid.

"Yes, Alceus. The Hetwan know we're tired," David said. "Withdraw a third of the men from the line. But first, gather the wounded. If they can walk, if they can limp, they're in the game. The one third plus the wounded, got me? Form them up right here. Fast! We'll launch a counterattack, off our left. We'll sweep around and try to cut them off. Go!"

He slapped the man on the shoulder.

"You're in charge?" Christopher asked. He'd joined us, looking about like the rest of us. Like the rest and relaxation at Olympus had never happened. "How did you manage that?"

"I just said, 'Athena has put me in charge,'" David said, obviously as amazed as any of us that such a simple declaration would work. "It helped that no one else was in charge. Ares and Heracles had been running the show, but as you know, Ares is off in a snit. And Heracles with him, I guess. Anyway, I haven't seen him. These guys were left here on their own."

"I thought they were enemies, those two," Christopher said. "Ares and Heracles? I mean, on the show . . ."

"I think the alliances change about every five minutes with these guys," Jalil said.

David nodded, but he wasn't paying attention. He was watching the gathering of his force. Men were dropping back and nearly dropping as they did so. They all seemed to have been injured. Red burn marks were on every arm and bare leg. Men were wobbly with exhaustion. The wounded were worse off still. At least one of them had very recently lost his arm at the elbow. The stump was tied off with a leather thong and crudely bandaged. The bandage was saturated with blood, dripping blood.

David shook his head disapprovingly, like a teacher facing a classroom of rowdy kids. "This isn't going to work, not over the long haul. The Hetwan don't retreat. You have to kill them. One by one. This isn't it. This isn't the way. Grab some more torches. Christopher and Jalil, I mean."

"*Ja wohl, mein* general," Christopher said and tried to snap his heels together.

It took me a second to realize that David was giving me an out.

"I can carry a torch," I said.

He grabbed my arm, but gently, with a bloody hand. "Look, April, this isn't some debate class discussion of women in combat. This is the real thing."

I pulled my arm away. I was angry. Not because

he'd offered me an out. I was angry because I wanted desperately to take it. I mean, how far was I going to carry my feminism? I'd done plenty. I'd held up my end.

"Hey, I've been in it this far. I'll grab a torch," I snapped, trying to use anger to mask my fear.

"Okay. They don't like fire. Or maybe it's the smoke. Either way, they don't like it."

"Very comforting," I mumbled inaudibly as I ran to make a torch. "Is there anyone who does like having a burning stick poked in their face?"

About three hundred men were formed up fairly tight by the time I got back with the torch. Alceus was with them. Christopher and Jalil were out front, holding six-foot-long torches like mine. David was talking to them in as loud a voice as he could manage.

"Don't stop to get into one-on-one fights. Move, move, move. We want to shock them, make them think we're a whole fresh force just coming in. And most of all we want to get behind them, trap them between our force and the main force. Everyone got that?"

I pushed through men twice my size to stand beside Christopher and Jalil.

"Did you hear General Custer's pep talk?" Christopher asked me.

"Yeah."

"The boy has found his true place in life,"
Christopher said, half admiring, half derisive. "In
case you were wondering, we're 'turning the enemy's line.'" He rolled his eyes.

David whipped out his sword and held it high
over his head. "Let's go!"

And suddenly I was running. Running as fast
as I could because if I slowed down about three
hundred Greeks were going to run right over me.

We raced along the back of our lines. All the way
to the end of the plateau. Then David swerved
sharply, plowing into and through the thinned-
out battle line of Greeks. I hesitated, unwilling to
risk jabbing my burning torch into the backs of
our own guys.

"Goddammit, don't slow down!" David yelled
directly at me, his face a freeze-frame amid chaos.

Some of the Greeks we ran into fell and were
trampled. Others caught up with us, and joined
the assault.

We burst through, to the front, and suddenly
there were Hetwan everywhere. I started screaming. Not scared screaming, wild, mad screaming. I
screamed in rage and ran, torch in the crook of
my right elbow, supported by my left hand. No
stopping. Run! Run straight at them, kill them,
kill them!

Something took over my brain. A lunatic shriek blanked out all thought. A siren in my head. A wail that was all, all my brain could produce. Ten thousand volts coursed through me. My feet flew. The torch was weightless. I no longer needed breath. I was transformed.

We hit the Hetwan without slowing. I aimed the burning end of my weapon straight for the closest Hetwan face. I hit him, collapsed his mouthparts. He fell back, beating the air with his weak arms.

I shoved the torch in, pushed with all my strength, grunting, crying, screaming all at once. Then one of our own slammed into my back, shot me forward. I kept my feet. Yes, move! Move!

I stabbed at another Hetwan. We were pushing through them, passing through them, tines of a pitchfork, splitting them up to be finished off by the men behind us.

The main body of our guys saw now what we were doing and started yelling, yelling and shouting and cheering. And I was cheering, too, yelling and shoving my flaming torch into Hetwan faces and bodies.

I felt the burn on my stomach. The Hetwan venom had penetrated my dress, burned through in an instant and was now burning into raw flesh just an inch from my navel. I slapped at it with my left hand and transferred some of the burn to my palm.

I bunched my dress fabric and scrubbed at the fire. The sizzling flame died, but the pain was only beginning.

The strangest feeling. I wished later I could remember the emotion. I wished I could get access to it, repeat it. It was the kind of thing an actress could use.

But I wasn't thinking about that. Wasn't thinking at all. I'd been in a transport of rage and fury, rushing to kill, driven to outrun my own fear.

But now something new and terrible rose up within me. Something so dark it was a black hole. Fear was gone. Pain was gone. I was gone, obliterated. No mind, no thought. A machine. A machine running on a power buried so far beneath civilized minds that people no longer know it's there.

I shoved my torch at the nearest Hetwan. He fired his venom. He missed. I didn't. I shoved the flaming end of the stick into his middle and spit at him, teeth bared, laughing.

I shoved and pulled back and stuck the flaming spear in his face. And I screamed, "Die! Die you ——!"

The Hetwan let loose the eerie Hetwan shriek

and I felt an obscene rush of triumph. Scream, you piece of crap.

I raised my spear over my head and shouted incoherent babble at the sky. Then I toppled off the plateau.

CHAPTER
XI

I fell, rolled, down and down, slamming rock and dirt. Down past levels of burning, charred steps and ladders. I was rolling down through the destruction caused by our earlier torches. Ashes in my mouth, fluttering ashes in the air.

Down toward the thousands of Hetwan who waited, blocked by the mess we'd made of their ladders.

I grabbed at dirt, tore my fingernails, scraped my face, slowed. Stopped.

For a long moment I lay there, frozen, breathing hard, choking on smoke. Then I looked up through stinging, weeping eyes. The plateau was far above me. I could see Hetwan and Greeks in battle. I saw swords flash. All so far away. The noise was so far away suddenly.

I was lying between two smoldering stairways.

My torch was gone. I had no weapons. Nothing. And the black rage was gone, evaporated. I felt pain in every part of my body.

I looked down and saw the Hetwan there. They stared up at me with malevolent insect eyes, their greedy mouthparts working as always. I was equidistant between the Hetwan below and those dying above. But the steepness of the hill kept the Hetwan at bay, at least as far as their climbing up after me. The Hetwan couldn't take the grade. I was beyond Super Soaker range.

I started climbing. Slid as much as I rose. Dug my sneaker toes into the crumbly dirt and tried to get traction. Tried to grab on with torn, bleeding fingers.

Then the Hetwan rose, a dozen or more. They flew. They flapped their wings and began to rise up after me. *Oh, God, I couldn't get away. Oh, God. They were going to kill me, like I had killed them.*

"Help!" I yelled. "Help! Help! David!"

The Hetwan flew slowly, but they didn't have far to fly. They loomed up, matching my height, then came in for the kill. I rolled onto my back, absurdly hoping to kick them away, but when I rolled over I slid down another ten feet.

Oh, God, face-to-face, I could see them, so close, ready to launch the burning wads that would eat into me, burn me alive, oh, God save me!

Suddenly an arrow appeared in the closest Hetwan. It simply appeared, sticking from his back between his wings. He fell. Fell and slammed into the ground just beside me.

I grabbed the body, grabbed the weak arm and a handful of crumpled wing, and with a burst of terror-strength rolled him over on top of me. Not a split second to spare. The Hetwan fired their venom. Numerous hits struck my dead Hetwan shield. I smelled burning bug.

The dead Hetwan's mouthparts were pressed against my face. They moved still, slowly, without force. I cowered and babbled and prayed, please save me, please let me live.

Arrows flew. Hetwan fell. But then, no more arrows. No more arrows, and still four Hetwan hovered within range, closing so they could get a shot around their dead comrade.

But again, arrows appeared. Someone above me had reloaded. Or a fresh archer had been brought up.

"April, stay down," I heard David yell from a million miles away.

I twisted my head and strained my eyes back to see up the slope. Three Greek archers stood at the edge of the drop. The battle up there was over. Now, a new battle. The battle for me.

The Hetwan knew they couldn't get enough of

their people up to the plateau to change matters up there, at least not now. But they could, by sacrificing more of their own, manage to kill me.

A second flight of a dozen Hetwan rose from down below. Down there they were out of range of the arrows. The archers could only hit them when they got close to me.

I stared down at them, down at the Hetwan spread across that lower plateau. So many. More of them than the Greeks had arrows. How long would I survive by hiding beneath a corpse?

Then a glimpse. Not so much of a thing as of a movement. A strange movement, something I'd seen before. Important. I strained to see. Yes, there, lurking within the endless ranks of Hetwan with their slidey-glidey movements, a different motion.

A Groucho walk. Alien, just as alien as the Hetwan, but not Hetwan. A creature shaped like a gray, oversized letter C, with a long, pointed snout surmounted by strange and beautiful eyes, deep red but with royal blue irises. They had four arms, two large and brawny, two smaller ones just below their eyes.

Not Hetwan. No, definitely not.

Coo-Hatch. I did not see their bird-sized, firefly juvenile phases flying around. At least two of the adults, though. Coo-Hatch, fighting alongside the Hetwan. The Coo-Hatch carried something between them. A tube. Gray metal. Fatter at one end, skinnier at the open end. A hollow tube with the hole an inch in diameter.

The Coo-Hatch used a long, thin rod to force a twisted paper wad down into the barrel. Then they dropped in a ball.

A gun. They had a gun. They were going to use it to kill me.

The Hetwan rose. Neared. The Greek arrows flew. Hetwan fell. And the Coo-Hatch below handed their now-loaded weapon to a team of four Hetwan who, with their weak limbs, could barely lift the gun. They steadied the weapon as well as they could.

A fifth Hetwan knelt behind the gun. I saw his insect eyes focus along the barrel's length. I saw the straight line from Hetwan eyes to barrel's end to me.

A sixth Hetwan appeared, carrying a burning match.

In seconds. They would fire in seconds.

Wait, April. Wait. Wait. Muscles as tight as steel bands. Wait. The match slowly nearing . . .

I jerked left, rolled from under my Hetwan shield.

The explosion was muffled. Not as loud as a gun should be. The bullet hit the dead Hetwan in the chest. I saw a puff of dirt. It had gone clean through. It would have gone clean through me.

Chaos below. The recoil of the gun had killed at least one of the firing team. The Coo-Hatch were stepping in to reload. More Hetwan flew toward more arrows. Just a matter of time. I couldn't climb. The gun would be reloaded, fired. How many more times could I fool them? Dodging bullets? Impossible.

"David, get me out of here!" I yelled.

"I think that's been arranged," David yelled back, strangely subdued.

I looked up, and there she was. She hovered in the air, so big, as big as her statue. Not a ghostly, special-effects apparition, but a real, immortal, flesh-and-blood creature who simply hung in the air. She reached down and closed her hand around my waist and raised me up.

She could have eaten me in two bites.

"You fight well," Athena said, her face filling my entire field of vision, widescreen.

"Thanks. But can we just get the hell out of here now?"

Chapter
XII

Saturday. The real world.

After the battle, after Athena picked me up and carried me away, I went back to what we now considered to be our house.

Jalil and Christopher came as well, but David stayed behind. He was Davideus now. He was General David. He had to get the Greeks ready for the next battle.

He'd given me a job to do as well. Figure out why the gods weren't in the fight directly. But I wasn't up for playing detective. I wasn't feeling well.

I went to my bed, freshly made of course, fell into it, and stared blankly at the walls for a while. I didn't feel anything. Not yet. But I sensed that within me, deep down inside, something was building. Something big. A wave that would sooner or later crash down on me and sweep me away.

After a while I fell asleep. Sleep is supposed to bring forgetfulness. Instead I crossed back over and rejoined myself, my true self, in the real world.

I was in church. Not a mass, just sitting in a pew, waiting for my turn in the confessional. A woman named Rebecca Burnside, twenty-something, in a conservative dress and brown hair that was wrong for the shape of her face, was sitting in the pew ahead of mine. She was turned around in her seat to talk to me.

I lost the train of what she was saying as the news update flooded my brain with the images I'd rather have forgotten. Men shouting. Swords. Smoky torches. Hetwan dying.

Images of myself, as though I'd been standing a little ways off, watching. Images of me wild, frenzied, murderous in a shredded dress and muddy sneakers.

I knew none of this. The last update from Everworld had me sated from a glorious dinner, falling into a plush bed. Since then the other me, that girl over in Everworld, had met Zeus, Apollo, Ares, Hera, Heracles, Artemis, and Athena.

Everworld me had flown on the back of a winged horse. And I/she had gone into desperate battle to save . . . To save what? The gods of Olympus? Those selfish, foolish, shortsighted creatures?

Or to avenge Ganymede? To simply stop Ka Anor and keep him from his goal? Why? Why had I fought? Why, when I fought, had I so lost myself?

"Don't you think?" Rebecca pressed. "I mean, maybe it's not that way for you."

I frowned. Tried to remember . . . What had we been talking about? What was the question? What trivial, minuscule conversation were we having?

The question was: Who was that girl with the torch, that girl filled with more rage than she had known existed? Who was that April?

"Yes," I guessed. "You're right."

Rebecca nodded. She spent a lot of time at church. She was in half a dozen church committees: altar guild, youth ministries, community outreach. She worked with the choir. Not as a singer — she didn't have the voice for it — but helping them with organization, ordering new gowns, passing out the sheet music.

I swear the woman confessed three times a week. What she confessed I couldn't imagine. As far as I knew, her life was spent entirely in the church or at her job with some insurance office.

What on earth had we been talking about?

"I mean, to me high school was a magical time. The friends I had then were the best friends I ever had."

Ah. That's what we were talking about. Of course. I'd already been bored and distracted when the news update had erased the last of my concentration.

How can I live like this? I wondered, angry at no one in particular, but focusing on poor Rebecca. How was I supposed to live simultaneously as a character in two very different movies? The other me was Sigourney Weaver in *Aliens*. The other me was in the middle of a film collaboration by Tim Burton and John Carpenter.

And over here I was in, what? Starring in *Pleasantville*? Living a black-and-white life without a splash of color?

No. That was wrong. This was my life. That place was my nightmare.

"Do you still see your high school friends?" I asked, struggling to be polite, forcing myself to concentrate.

"Oh, some. I mean here, for example. I see some in church. Some of the girls from the good old days."

"But you don't hang out? Do you go to one another's homes and, I don't know, whatever? Hang out? Go to movies? Go out to dinner?"

Her smug face fell and I was instantly sorry for the question. I'd been carelessly unkind. My mind off somewhere else. And yet, I discovered that I really wanted to know the answer.

"I see the old gang around. Here in church. Oh, just yesterday I saw my best friend Ellen in Whole Foods, at the cheese counter. But you know, they mostly have jobs or else families."

I realized I was staring at her. A pink blush climbed up her neck. I didn't want to embarrass her, but suddenly what she was saying seemed terribly important. Why would she go on about how great high school was, why would she talk about these deep friendships, when it was obvious that those friendships had died within minutes of graduation?

It was my turn to say something. Rebecca glanced toward the ratty curtain of the old-fashioned, carved walnut confessional.

"I have lots of friends," I said, failing to come up with anything better. "I mean, at school. I have lots of friends."

"You're drama club, right?" she asked, as though she were up on all the current cliques.

"Yes. I mean, I know, I know how dorky it sounds to say you want to be an actor when you're still in school. But that is what I want to do."

She nodded. Her eyes became completely

opaque. She was putting up a wall between us. Defending herself. I wanted to ask her why she'd lost all her friends. I wanted to know if it was something she'd done, or something she'd become, or was it just inevitable.

I wanted to ask her if she had dreamed of being a secretary in an insurance office. And what she confessed three times a week.

"Ah. Your turn," she said, smiling with relief and nodding toward the confessional, now available.

"You can go first if —"

"No, no, I'm in no hurry," she said. And then she shot me a poisonous look, as if I had accused her of something.

"Thanks." I left her. Crossed the church doing the "pew walk," a sideways kind of move where you could fall over at any moment.

I sat down in the quiet booth and drew the curtain.

I could see Father Mike through the screen. He was taking a few quick drags on a cigarette, sucking the smoke deep. Then reluctantly he ground it out in an unseen ashtray.

"Sorry," he muttered. "I'm on the patch. You can see how well it's working."

"Ego te absolvo," I said. Latin for "I absolve you."

"I think that's my line," he said dryly.

I went into the usual litany of venial sins: disrespect of my parents; anger; a possible cheating incident where I innocently and accidentally saw an answer on someone else's paper, and it was different from the answer I was going to give, and I used the answer I'd seen.

"Did you intend to cheat?"

"No. But I used the answer."

"Was it the right answer?"

"Actually no."

"Then I think that one took care of itself. Go on."

I hesitated. I had confessed all I could remember of transgressions here in the real world. But what about her? What about Everworld me?

"I have a hypothetical question," I said.

"Oh?" He shifted in his seat. Bored? Or did this interest him more than my list of no-big-deal sins?

"It's, um, it has to do with this story I read. A short story. Do you have the time?"

"I have time. Shoot."

"Okay. In this story this person, this character, he's got a kind of . . . kind of a Dr. Jekyll and Mr. Hyde thing. You know, he's split in two. And the good part of him goes to confession and confesses all the stuff he did. He himself, I mean, not his other half." I sighed. Yeah, this sounded believable. "Anyway, Dr. Jekyll confesses for Dr. Jekyll. But he's also Mr. Hyde, right? I mean, Hyde is part of him, but only a part, so he seems different. Like he's existing in a parallel universe or something. So what about the things Mr. Hyde does? Should Dr. Jekyll confess for Mr. Hyde? And if he doesn't, can Jekyll still take communion?"

"That's the question?"

"Yes. Hypothetically."

"Hmmm. I don't know. It comes down to the question of whether Jekyll and Hyde are really one person or two. If Hyde is a separate person then how can Jekyll confess for him? But if Hyde is really Jekyll then Jekyll has to confess the sins he committed as Hyde. Good grief. You want something more than that, you're going to have to ask the bishop. Or go talk to the chair of the theology department at the university."

"Thanks," I said.

"Okay. Anything more?"

"There is one thing more. Lying."

"You already confessed to lying."

"I may have lied again since then," I said.

XIII

I met Magda and Alison at Old Orchard Mall, at the Barnes and Noble there. Old Orchard is an outdoor mall. Like a regular mall, sort of, but without a roof over the walkways.

It was raining intermittently, drizzling from a gray-on-gray sky. So for once, despite the fact that it was Saturday, there was parking, at least out on the fringes.

We were on a mission to buy me some sweaters — Fields had a sale — and Alison some shoes.

We had to scurry from store to store, trying to dodge the raindrops, trying not to accept the fact that autumn was full upon us and already threatening us with the unavoidable, and unavoidably painful, Chicago winter.

Everworld me was sleeping. Presumably. I was never sure. I felt, vaguely sometimes, that I could tell when that part of me awoke, and "I" crossed back over. But the fact was, whether Everworld April woke or slept, I would remain here. I would still be shopping, still be with my friends. Still be noticing the fact that all the flower beds were filled with nothing but wet dirt, that the sun was lower than it should be at noon, that summer was over, over, over and even fall was ending all too quickly.

"You are so perky today, April. Miss Sunshine," Magda said as we trailed behind Alison in the Nordstrom's shoe department. "Are those Mephistos?"

"You're being sarcastic?" I said.

"About the shoes? No. About the state of your perkiness, yeah."

"I'm perky," I said.

"No, you're dark, gloomy, oppressed, preoccupied, possibly even suffering from PMS."

"Hey, I'm gloomy, not bitchy. Does anyone still wear heels like that?"

"Sure. Twenty-two-year-old wives of fifty-year-old millionaire husbands looking to spark up the nocturnal action."

I laughed. Magda is a deliberately, calculatedly

provocative person. She'd said this in a voice just loud enough to be heard by a hard-eyed twenty-ish trophy wife in a full-length fur coat.

Magda and Alison are both drama club. Alison is a willowy blond who looks like she survived a brush with anorexia. She has a face made for magazine covers, and moist brown eyes that look as if they're always either just about to cry or just stopped crying. She will never be able to play a comedic role. That's what I tell myself whenever I'm overcome with resentment at her ability to eat soft pretzels, doughnuts, hot dogs, and pizza and not gain an ounce.

"Very discreet," I commented as we cruised past the fur coat.

"I thought so. So, why are you all Dostoyevsky today? Talk to me. Get in touch with your inner Ibsen, your deepest, darkest Ingmar Bergman."

Magda could probably play any role. She was playing a role right now, had been as long as I've known her. She played the world-weary, know-it-all cynic with the overactive libido. And yet, when she wanted examples of things depressive and gloomy she whipped out Dostoyevsky and Ibsen. Still, she never seemed at all phony to me. That's how good she was: She could play a role, let you know she was playing a role, and through it all seem authentic.

Meanwhile Alison had snagged a clerk and was showing him the three shoes she was carrying. Then she spotted someone she knew, a guy, gave us a cool "go away for five minutes" look, and drifted off, laughing and tossing her hair.

"Who is that guy? Do you know him?" I asked.

"Mmm, no. Not my type. Alison loves those girly-looking guys, doesn't she? That guy looks like Jesus."

"Magda, you have no idea what Jesus looks like."

"Sure I do. Christian Bale. In that lame miniseries? But don't try to distract me. What's the existential angst thing today?"

I sighed. "I saw this woman today who was unhappy, I think, because she lost all her high school friends. Or maybe she lost all her friends because she was unhappy."

"Wow, you got all this just by looking at someone? How about these?" Magda held up a pair of boots.

"Would they be for me, for you, or for someone named Bambi who has a live Web-cam in her bedroom?"

Magda put the boots down. "Where was this, your fateful meeting with the friendless woman?"

"Confession."

"Ah. Boy, I'll bet the priests really look forward

to your confession every week. They've got to be thinking, *'Man, this girl never gets any action.'* Did you confess your impure thoughts about Ben Affleck? Or was it just the usual chronic, sinful failure to scrape all your dishes before you put them in the sink?"

"Just don't you ever start going, Magda. I don't want to have to follow you onstage, so to speak."

She laughed. Proudly, of course. "So you're thinking, I invest all my energy in my friends and maybe in a year and a half when I graduate that'll be it. Friends all gone."

"Yeah," I said. "That. Plus the fact that it's fall and there's no sunlight and pretty soon it's going to be ten degrees below zero with a thirty-mile-an-hour wind and big piles of dirty snow everywhere and my feet all cold and my face all chapped."

"There's Thanksgiving. And Christmas. Plus lots of people stay in touch with high school friends. My mom is still best friends with her best friend from high school."

"It's a stupid thing to worry about," I said. "Okay, all done being gloomy." I twisted a finger into my cheek to make a dimple.

Alison reappeared. "Where's that clerk?"

"Maybe he had to heave up his lunch after

watching you drool all over that guy," Magda suggested.

"He was cute, though, huh?"

"Absolutely," Magda responded enthusiastically. "I like a guy with lots of ear hair."

"I was not talking about the clerk," Alison said. "God, you are so jealous when any guy doesn't look at you."

"Oh, he checked me out," Magda said smugly.

"No, he didn't." Alison looked at me for confirmation.

"I gave him one of these," Magda said and arched her back, pushing her Miracle Bra cleavage out. "He looked."

Alison laughed, which scrunched up her sad eyes and transformed her entire face. So maybe she could play comedy someday.

And I felt a wave of . . . of what? Of several feelings at once. The sadness you feel when you know you are happy, but don't expect it to last. Wistful, I guess. Stupid. All because of some lonely woman in church? That wasn't me. That wasn't going to be me.

Great goal, I told myself sardonically. *Aim high! Don't become Rebecca Burnside. Wow, there's an accomplishment.*

We headed back out, into a steady drizzle. We

walked, huddled together against the damp and cold, clinging to the safe spaces beneath overhanging awnings. We joked and gossiped and laughed.

This was my life. This was what I was worried about losing, this closeness. This was the definition of my life to this point, and as I drifted into and out of Magda's running commentary on the people we passed, I found myself thinking, *I wonder what's going on over there?*

I wonder what's happening to me over there?

CHAPTER
XIV

"Get up. Come on, wake up."

I opened my eyes. David was shaking me.

"You look like old kitty litter," I said, blinking my eyes to clear away the sleep.

He needed a shave, which was nothing new except that he'd shaved the last time I'd seen him. How much time had passed? He was dirty, sweaty. The toga was gone. He was back in his own clothes.

"What's the matter?" I asked and sat up.

"What's the matter? Less than was the matter, but still plenty. I've got guys out drafting everyone who can walk. They've got thousands of refugees hiding in caves around the back side of the mountain, just sitting there doing nothing. Plus the villagers on the south slope. Well,

they're in the army now. And my man Hephaistos and I have some things cooking up."

I looked closely at him. Exhausted, yes. But he
was exalted, too. There was a fanatic's light burning in his bleary, red-rimmed eyes. However long
I'd been asleep, he'd been awake.

"Okay. Good. I'm awake. I can help. Sorry, I
just fell asleep."

"That's okay, I've got it under control. I've got
some guys I think I can trust handling the details.
No help from the gods, of course, except for Hephaistos, who's cool. The rest, they won't take orders from a mortal."

I climbed out of my soft, soft bed. I was still
wearing the ragged dress. There were stains striped
all down the front. Dark red. And a green so dark it
was almost black.

Blood. Human and Hetwan.

"Where are Christopher and Jalil?"

"Getting dressed. Turns out there are other op-
tions besides togas. They have these kinds of leg-
gings, strap-up kinds of deals. Plus they washed
our clothes for us. The Greeks may not mind
fighting in miniskirts, but it's really not me."

Two servants appeared. One carried a massive
tray piled with food. The other carried dry, neatly
stacked clothing of various types.

"The Hetwan have asked for a parley. We have

a truce till their representatives can get here. They can't fly this high, so we're bringing them through the lines. Blindfolded. I don't want the bastards reporting back on our preparations."

He was talking to himself more than to me. Rattling away at a mile a minute. High on adrenaline. High on power.

"Come on, let's go," he prodded.

"How about turning your back while I change?"

"Oh. Okay, yeah."

I slipped off the bloody rags and, with the help of the female servant, dressed. My look was more Artemis now. My legs were covered, my neckline was no longer precarious. I had my own underthings back, all clean. A luxury, although I couldn't erase from my mind the very recent memories of cruising Banana Republic with Magda and Alison: all that clean, clean, new and normal clothing.

"Okay, let's go," I said. I glanced at the pile of rags I was leaving behind. Tried not to think of what those stains meant. And I tried, too, not to acknowledge how proud I was to have fought and survived.

This time there was no long walk to Zeus's palace. Pegasus, Pelias, and the others were waiting. Christopher and Jalil were already mounted.

"Hey, Pelias," I said.

We mounted up, a bit less awkwardly this time.

The horses broke into a run, then began flapping their wings. We reached the great open hall in minutes. The winged steeds circled down to land just off the gods' platform.

This time there were fewer gods present. Artemis, Apollo, Athena, Hera, Dionysus, Hermes, and a strange god I hadn't noticed before. He had a huge upper body, arms like bridge cables, a chest that looked like it might have been built of cinderblocks. But his legs were shrunken, undersized. Almost a child's legs, surely incapable of carrying his bulk. His face was dark, deeply tanned, as though he spent all his life in the sun. When he glanced at me I saw fire, literal fire, burning where his irises should have been.

"That's Heph," David said. "Hephaistos. God of fire or whatever. He's the only one of these gods aside from Athena who is any damn use at all. He handles weapons. I have him and his boys making swords and shields for the draftees. He's cool. Crippled, though. Lame."

"Shouldn't we say he's 'differently abled'?" Christopher asked in a mocking whisper.

"Heph calls himself lame, which is good enough for me," David answered. "He's the only one of these guys who actually has a job besides sitting around drinking, screwing, and bitching all day."

"There: You have described my career aspirations," Christopher said. "Should have taken that immortality thing."

David's deference toward the gods had obviously taken a beating while I slept. Familiarity was breeding contempt.

Zeus was not an eagle at the moment. Nor a wise old man. He was a monstrous, sleek bull with horns you could use to stretch a clothesline.

"What's with the bull?" Christopher asked.

"I think he meets and greets that way," Jalil said. "It's that whole mortals-bursting-into-flame thing. He has to reveal himself slowly. W.T.E.," he added as a commentary.

Welcome To Everworld.

The horses flew away once they'd dropped us off. Artemis spared me a languid look. I had the sense that she was a bit annoyed that I was dressed like her. A pair of nymphs were feeding her grapes and tiny cakes shaped like deer.

Four big men in armor came in, led by a pair of servants. The four men in turn were leading two blindfolded Hetwan.

I felt a visceral distaste for the aliens. Hard not to. They had tried repeatedly to kill me. And there was still Ganymede, a memory burned into my memory.

"Remove their blindfolds," Athena said.

The goddess of wisdom and war took a central position between Zeus and the Hetwan. The Hetwan stood there patiently, showing no sign that they were the least bit nervous or afraid.

The blindfolds fell away. The Hetwan did not blink their big dragonfly eyes.

"Speak your message, Hetwan. Speak it quickly lest our patience wear thin and we cast you down from this mountain," Athena said with all the haughtiness of a woman who has nothing to fear.

"You may kill us or not, as is your wish," one of the Hetwan said in the whispery, softly musical Hetwan voice. "My death is irrelevant. I serve Ka Anor."

"Speak your message," Athena said, abandoning both the threats and the formal speech.

"I come to speak the words of Ka Anor to the gods of Olympus. Ka Anor says the following: The treaty of peace between us may be resumed under certain conditions."

Zeus was morphing slowly again, becoming less bull and more Sean Connery. He looked sharply at the Hetwan, horns jerking across a wide arc. His hope was all too obvious.

Athena kept a better poker face. "What conditions?"

"Zeus will retain Olympus as his home and will

be safe within his mountain fastness. He may keep with him as companions any five gods he may choose. All other gods of Olympus, and all gods residing in the countryside around Olympus, will be given to Ka Anor."

The Hetwan fell silent.

Athena started to speak, but Zeus rode right over her. "What guarantees does Ka Anor give?"

"As a sign of Ka Anor's sincerity he will order the deaths of five thousand Hetwan within sight of Olympus."

I wanted to laugh. It was absurd. It was monstrous. Ka Anor was asking for the gods of Olympus to be turned over en masse? For Zeus to betray his own children so that he himself might survive?

"Five thousand deaths? Surely a good token. But five gods as companions?" Zeus repeated skeptically. "That is far too few. Ka Anor asks too much. Shall I purchase my safety at the cost of my own children? What of my loneliness here? Five companions? No. It is far too few."

He was bargaining!

I saw a dark, murderous look in Athena's eyes. But I also saw defeat there. She expected this transparent ploy to work. She knew, deep in her heart, that Zeus would sell out his own.

The other gods stirred nervously. Glanced

around at one another. They, too, were looking to maneuver. Not expecting Zeus to tell the Hetwan to drop dead, but preparing to jockey for one of the favored slots.

"Surely the five would be chosen from among the twelve great gods," Apollo said. "And surely those who have already fled or sit pouting in their temples, such as Ares, surely they would not be among the five."

It was amazing. As horrible as it was, I wanted to laugh. The Hetwan had taken the measure of these spoiled, weak immortals. Ka Anor had, with absolute contempt, split his enemy into factions. The gods would fight one another to be among the five.

"It's a trick," Athena grated. "Can you not see that this is a trick, Great Father? Ka Anor hopes to divide us. He would have you cut off both arms and then trust his mercy."

"Are you afraid, Athena?" Zeus asked scornfully. "Do you doubt that you would win my favor and be among the five?"

Insane. They were insane. Only a mad fool could fall for this.

"Trojan horse," Jalil whispered to me.

I knew what he meant. When we had first come to Everworld we'd discovered that the residents were not exactly skeptical. They tended to believe first and doubt only much later. Jalil had cited the Trojan horse story. Odysseus had hidden his Greeks inside a hollow wooden horse that the Trojans then, with jaw-dropping naivete, dragged inside the secure walls of their city. At night the Greeks emerged, opened the gates, and let their army in to slaughter the Trojans.

The gods of Olympus were fickle, selfish, and cruel. They were also as naive as a four-year-old sitting on Santa's lap.

I heard a low growl. It was coming from David.

"Don't be a damned idiot," David erupted. "I mean, can you possibly be this stupid?"

He was yelling at Zeus. Yelling at one of the greatest gods of Everworld.

"You think they'd be here bargaining at all if they could beat us? Ka Anor is worried. He'll give up five thousand Hetwan? Big deal, we'll kill a lot more than that before they make it up this mountain, and Ka Anor knows it."

I cringed, expecting the thunderbolt.

But Jalil stepped in to deflect Zeus's attention. "Great Zeus, Father Zeus, I don't see any reason for you to trust Ka Anor. Didn't he just violate the last treaty you had with him?"

"Silence, mortals," Zeus thundered, and a lightning bolt appeared in his hand. "This does not concern you. This is a matter for the gods to decide."

"Go ahead and hit me with the thunderbolt!" David yelled, stalking toward the platform and slashing at the air with sharp, sudden gestures. "But until you fry me I'm going to tell you how it is. You're being taken for a fool. Ka Anor is going to kill and eat every last god in Everworld. This deal is pure bull. He's got you doing his killing for him. He'll keep you alive till you feed him all your children, all your so-called companions, one by one, then he'll come for you."

That almost seemed to penetrate Zeus's head. Almost. He shot a sharp look at the Hetwan spokesman. "Is this true? Does Ka Anor plan to betray me?"

"Jesus H.," Christopher muttered in disgust. "Do you think?"

The Hetwan ambassador said, "Ka Anor will keep his word."

Then, for the first time, the other Hetwan spoke up. But the voice was not the flutey, whispery Hetwan voice. It was the voice of a girl. A voice that sent a jolt through me.

I did a literal double take. Looked, looked away, looked back. The Hetwan was changing.

"Ka Anor thinks you are a weak fool, Great Zeus. It is just the way this mortal has said: Ka Anor will eat you, too. And soon."

The gods stared. But so did we all.

I knew the voice. So did David, and he seemed to be frozen stiff, his mobile rage turned to stiff confusion.

Only slowly did recognition come to Jalil and Christopher, and by then the "Hetwan" was disappearing, to be replaced by a striking, if not really beautiful girl with blond hair and full lips and cold gray eyes.

"Senna," Christopher said.

The Hetwan, the real one, jerked in surprise. I hadn't known Hetwan could be surprised.

"Senna," David said, almost sobbing the word.

She sent him a slight smile. "General David. I told you. I warned you the day would come. And now, here you are."

"Yeah," he said faintly.

He seemed to shrink before my eyes. A wax man in an oven. Davideus was a wounded teenager again.

"Who is this?" Zeus asked guardedly. "Who is this seeming mortal who can change shape and appearance like a god?"

"The witch, of course," Athena said. She was interested but not impressed. As though a witch, while someone to treat with respect, was no possible threat. "You hid yourself among the Hetwan, witch?"

"My name is Senna Wales."

"And mine is Athena, witch. Do not anger me."

Senna wavered. Nothing anyone but me would notice. But I sensed she'd just figured out that Athena was out of her league.

"Yes, Athena. I hid myself among the Hetwan. I have been trying to reunite with these, my friends." She waved her hand to encompass the four of us.

Christopher snorted. Loudly enough to be heard by all. Senna gritted her teeth. A muscle in her jaw twitched. She was not her usual calm and in-control self. She must have had a bad time of it with the Hetwan.

"I was trying to catch up to my friends, but they moved quickly. Once they joined with Dionysus and Ganymede I followed at a safe distance. But they lost me at the city of Ka Anor, where I was discovered and taken prisoner. I escaped, but not before my friends, too, had escaped from the city. I was trapped when the Hetwan army began to reinforce its position here at Olympus. Since then I have passed as one of them."

"It's a brave tale," Apollo said.

"The courage of a man," Artemis remarked. "A courage men claim and believe is theirs alone. I think I like you, witch. You are lovely as well as brave. And dangerous, I think," she added with a smirk.

"I hope I am dangerous to the enemies of Olympus," Senna said, as smooth as a United Nations diplomat.

"What's your game?" Jalil asked her bluntly.

She shrugged. "I've come to warn Great Zeus that Ka Anor's offer is a trap."

"Yeah, great insight there," Christopher said with a laugh. "A monkey could see that."

I saw him go white as he realized what he'd said. But Zeus either didn't get the insult or was too preoccupied to fly into a rage.

Zeus glared at the genuine Hetwan. He rose up to his full height, a giant among giants. And suddenly the lightning reappeared in his right hand. And black clouds began boiling into view above us.

"Go, Hetwan. Return to your master. And tell him that Zeus is no fool. Tell Ka Anor this: I am Zeus, who slew the Titans. I am Zeus, who holds sway over all the gods of Olympus. I am Zeus, who took and held this mountain against the onslaught of that Roman pretender, Jupiter, and his brood."

A sudden movement and the lightning snapped. It struck just in front of the Hetwan.

The marble exploded in a shower of splinters. The Hetwan staggered back, covering his eyes from the flash.

"I am Zeus!" he bellowed in a voice that must have been heard by Ka Anor himself, miles away and buried within his needle tower at the center of his impassable crater domain.

"I am Zeus, who in the dark mists of time united all the many great gods of all the great nations together to create Everworld out of nothingness. Tell Ka Anor that Great Zeus will not be frightened. Tell Ka Anor that Mighty Zeus still reigns atop Olympus and will do so till the foundation stones of the world crack and crumble to dust. Now go."

He fired another lightning bolt that singed the Hetwan and rocked the vast hall with explosive thunderclaps.

The Hetwan stood. Very still. Unconcerned. Almost bored. And then, slowly, turned and slidey-glideyed away.

Zeus subsided. The black clouds rolled away, leaving pure blue behind.

It was an amazing performance. It was impossible not to feel renewed energy and determination. It was impossible not to feel a surge of optimism.

David stood tall again. Apollo smiled. Hermes

was grinning, Artemis, too, although hers was a more sardonic look. Hera watched, waited, seemed to be in her own little world.

Only Athena remained unimpressed. That bothered me. But what bothered me more was what happened next.

"Now what do we do?" Zeus asked, almost pitifully. "Now what do we do?"

Hera spoke. "What of Athena's hero? This Davideus? Is he not to save us? Or will he simper and mewl for this witch?"

David heard his own name and looked around like a man caught napping in an important meeting. He shook his head slightly, perplexed.

Hermes laughed. "What a pity that Aphrodite is not here. She could test her powers of enchantment against this witch's. Poor mortal, one almost pities him: a hero laid low by the wiles of a witch."

Senna absorbed the indirect praise. She concealed the shrewd look, hid her satisfaction. "David . . . I mean, Davideus will stop the Hetwan. He will be your hero. If I choose. I have my own powers. My own wisdom."

Athena nodded. "You have a price?"

"Yes," Senna said, not embarrassed.

"Name it."

"Two things. First, sanctuary while I stay at Olympus."

Athena looked inquiringly at her father.

"Granted," Zeus said.

"And one other thing," Senna said. "I have escaped Loki thus far. But I have another foe, more dangerous because he is more patient. A wizard. A sorcerer. He pursues me, not just in his own form, but with beasts and birds who are his friends. The price for my help is his imprisonment or death, should he ever come here."

"And who is this sorcerer?"

"His name is Merlin."

"Done," Athena said, not even waiting for Zeus. "But I add one condition of my own: Davideus is my hero. I am a jealous goddess. I will not share. Release him. Release him fully, witch, and do not attempt to deceive me. My eyes are not easily fooled. I will protect you while you are here, and I will seize this wizard should he ever come. But you will release Davideus. And know this, witch: If you refuse, it will be you who is chained, as Prometheus was bound. Chained to a wall, and an eagle sent each day to rip out your living organs, never to die, each day to be reborn and ripped apart afresh."

Senna swallowed hard. The smug look was gone. She glanced at David.

Then she said, "He is free."

XVI

I had done nothing. Said nothing. I'd stood silent and powerless as first Zeus and the Hetwan ambassador, then my half sister and the goddess Athena had tossed our lives back and forth between them like kids playing a game of catch.

Now it was over. We were dismissed. The gods needed a revel.

Zeus was bellowing for wine and mead and the finest delicacies, as well as for the nymphs and satyrs and musicians and dancers. Dionysus was shouting happy directions to Hebe, the young goddess who took Ganymede's place as immortal bartender when he wasn't present. She had the job permanently now.

Senna walked ahead of us. As though she were leading us. As though she were in charge. But Athena had gotten the better of her and I could see the pink blush of Senna's icy rage. Once more she'd been forcibly reminded that when she played with the gods she was playing out of her league.

And she didn't like that. Senna had always had a high opinion of herself. But it seemed to me that Everworld had made her openly arrogant, something I'd not seen growing up with her.

Pegasus, Pelias, and the others waited to carry us back to our temporary home. But none of them would carry Senna. We flew. She traveled by chariot below us.

Back at our Motel 6 Olympus home the servants brought food into the pentagonal open-air courtyard. I was starving. Any meeting with gods is nerve-racking. Stress will give you an appetite. They brought wine, too, and Christopher downed two bowls before David or anyone else had time to raise an objection.

"Wasn't bad enough, now we've got Senna back with us?" Christopher demanded. Then he grinned. "Although, old Athena witch-slapped her, didn't she? I'm getting so I kind of like her. For a god, she's not all bad."

"They're all bad," Jalil said. "They're bad no matter if they're for us or against us. Power corrupts. They can't stop themselves from messing up people's lives, it's all they have going on.

Don't count on Athena. She's still a god and all gods are rotten."

"They aren't gods," I said. "There's only one God. They can call themselves gods but that's not what they are. They may be immortals. Call them whatever, but these creatures aren't related to God."

Jalil took that as a challenge, and I guess he and I were both frustrated enough to cut loose. Jalil gets snake's eyes when he's mad, and his voice can be witheringly sarcastic.

"Yeah, like your God never does insane things for insane reasons? What's all that fire and brimstone about? What's all that 'slay all the Canaanites' stuff?"

"He died for our sins," I said. "Can you see Zeus or Huitzilopoctli or even Athena doing that?"

"Kind of a temporary death, though, huh?" Jalil sneered. "Doesn't really count. Hey, I'll die for you if you tell me I can pop back up, good as new, three days later."

"My God loves me," I said. "That's the difference. Humans are nothing but toys for these so-called gods, these immortals."

"And that's not —" Jalil began.

"Whoa! Whoa!" Christopher held up his hands and stepped between us, sloshing a little wine as he did so. "Don't go all Bosnia on us here, you two. Boy, it's sad when I have to be the voice of reason. I mean, come on, look at all that food just sitting there. We have problems, kids — let's put the whole pay-per-view of Darwin-versus-the-pope thing aside. Look: They have those poppy seed cakes."

"Darwin versus the pope?" Jalil echoed incredulously.

"Live and let live. Peace, baby. Do your own thing. Find your own bliss," Christopher said.

"That must be strong wine," I muttered, glancing at Jalil to see if we were making up.

"And a little drunk shall lead them," Jalil said.

Just then Senna arrived. She looked a bit windblown, but then I guess we all did.

I shot a look at David. So did Senna. Her expression was unreadable. Her emotions carefully concealed.

David watched her in wonder. Not amazed at her, but amazed at some memory. Embarrassed, it seemed to me. And a little angry.

Was he really free of her enchantment? Maybe. Maybe free of the part that was magic. But beyond the witch's trickery she still had her face, her eyes, her body, and her strange, strong, compelling mind. She still carried the promise of hopeless infatuation.

She embodied the lost cause, the empty promise

of futility and disappointment and frustration that I guess attracts some men. Senna was still the woman of ice who would never, ever be thawed.

"Well, General David," Senna snapped. "I am at your command, it seems. What do you want to know?"

Christopher grinned, hugely pleased to see Senna at least temporarily brought low. "Hey, Senna. Have a muffin."

David and Senna both ignored him. "Tell me about the Coo-Hatch," he said to Senna.

"So. You know about that?"

I said, "I saw them. I saw a team of Coo-Hatch loading and preparing some kind of heavy gun or small cannon. They gave it to the Hetwan to fire. I think it killed one of the Hetwan who fired it, but it also killed at least one of the Greeks earlier and almost killed me."

Senna nodded. "Yes, the Coo-Hatch won't fire the things themselves. They won't kill for Ka Anor. They don't like Ka Anor, at least that's what I hear."

"So why are they supplying advanced weapons to the Hetwan?" Jalil asked.

Senna raised an eyebrow. "I don't read minds, Jalil. Let me have one of those small loaves of bread there. Hand it to me, if you would. I know your hands are clean."

Jalil had begun to comply. He hesitated, executed a sort of motion-stutter when she said his hands were clean. He clenched his jaw and grabbed the loaf.

She smirked as if she had just scored a win of some sort.

What was it between those two? What was the thing she had over him?

She ripped the loaf open and took a bite. "I don't know why the Coo-Hatch are there. Maybe you should ask Athena. She knows more than she tells you people, you can be sure of that."

"Maybe so," Jalil said. "But then, so do you. You lie. You deceive. And even when you tell the truth you can shade it, spin it so that it's nothing but another lie. You should go into politics."

If Senna had intimidated Jalil it hadn't lasted.

"We're in a war here," David said. "The Hetwan are coming after Olympus with everything they've got. And they've got plenty. The Greeks are down to a relative handful of men. The Hetwan aren't good at war, they're not experienced, you can see that in the way they attack straight on at the first available place. But they don't scare. And for some reason we never quite figure out, these idiot gods either can't or won't get in the fight."

"They fight by proxy," Jalil said. "You go back

through mythology, the gods are always using humans. That was the Trojan War. Bunch of Greek gods on the side of Troy, a bunch of other Greek gods on the other side. They support their heroes, and they help mess up some other god's boy."

I said, "But Athena at least realizes that's not working now. I mean, none of these gods backs the Hetwan, do they?"

I looked at Senna, I don't know why. Maybe because to me she seemed to be at least halfway over the line between mortal and immortal. That was no compliment.

"I don't think we get it," Jalil said. "They're immortal. They live forever. Politics, backbiting, shafting one another, this is the game they know. What they don't know is survival. That's a human thing. If you think you're going to live forever you don't spend a lot of time figuring out how to stay alive."

Senna nodded. She started to say something, hesitated, looked at each of us in turn, and I guess decided to go ahead. "Look, you guys think I'm just power hungry or something? You think I've lost it, having delusions of grandeur? I knew, or at least guessed, sensed that I'd be carried to Everworld. They needed me. Or someone like me. Why? Because the gods are all-powerful?" She shook her head and answered her own question.

"Why would Loki need me if the gods are all-powerful?"

She suddenly threw out her hands and formed tight little fists, like some parody of a mad dictator. "They're weak! They're slow and stupid and rigid. Yeah, they have power, but they have no idea how to use it."

She stabbed a finger at Jalil. "You're so smart, Jalil. Tell me: Who is the most powerful individual in Everworld? Zeus? Odin? Quetzalcoatl? Amon-Ra? Hel? That clown of a dragon, Nidhoggr?"

"I don't know," Jalil admitted.

"Don't you? Let me tell you, Jalil, you've met the most powerful individual in Everworld. And he's not a god."

"Merlin?" I said.

Senna glared at me, eyes narrow and mean. "Yes. Merlin. The old wizard. The old man in the funny hat. Merlin. Why? Because he has magic? Yes, but his magic is nothing compared to Zeus's raw power. Merlin has human ingenuity. Human flexibility." She tapped a finger to her temple. "Merlin has imagination."

"And so do you," I said, seeing where she was going now. "You have magic. And you have imagination. As well as ambition."

"Yeah," she said, smiling like the girl I'd known

most of my life. "See, I'm not so crazy, sister. My powers barely exist in the real world. They're shadows of what I can do here. Back there what could I ever be? What's my highest possible ambition, back there in the real world? Get a good job?" She laughed. "Here I can be Merlin. And I can be more than Merlin. I have an advantage, even over Master Merlin the Magnificent."

She ate another few bites of the bread, eyes downcast, waiting. Waiting for what? For us to figure out what her advantage was?

It hit me all at once. A sudden, total, undeniable realization.

"Us. We're the advantage you have. That's why you drew us to the lake. You hoped we'd do just what we did: try to save you and be carried across with you. But you miscalculated there, didn't you?" I said proudly. "We didn't follow your orders."

Jalil laughed, not unkindly. "She didn't need us to follow orders, April. She knew we wouldn't. That was her edge. She knew we'd try to stay alive, and she knew we'd do damage in the process. Throw things off. Mess up plans. We're a wild card. But a wild card that Senna can predict, at least a little. Totally unpredictable to Merlin or the gods."

"Like loaded dice," Christopher marveled, nodding at Jalil. "It's not that she knows exactly how we'll roll, but she knows the odds of how we'll roll. And Merlin and Loki and all don't have that edge."

Senna was enjoying the stares of awe and outrage. She swallowed and tossed the loaf aside and brushed her hands. "And look what's happened so far: Loki's plan foiled; Huitzilopoctli weakened; Merlin deprived forever of Galahad, his strong right arm; and now Ka Anor is stymied at the gates of Olympus."

Before any of us could do anything — and choking her came to mind — a servant rushed in.

"Pardon, mighty Davideus. From the camp, they've sent word with Pegasus. The Hetwan are preparing to attack again."

CHAPTER
XVII

In the blink of an eye General Davideus was back. The diminished, witch-spelled David was gone.

"Okay. Here's what we have: I've had my boys drafting men out of the villages on the south slope. So we'll have another thousand, fifteen hundred men. Not trained, but that's okay, the Hetwan aren't exactly great swordsmen. And Hephaistos has the weapons ready. He's also built two catapults I designed for him. They aren't state-of-the-art but they'll throw ten pounds of burning volcanic stone over the heads of our boys and burn the Hetwan assault platforms again, keep them from reinforcing. That's part one."

"A god who works?" Jalil asked.

"He's the lame one I pointed out to you. Can't

walk," David explained. "So I made a deal with him. A bit of new-to-Everworld technology.

"Anyway, that's part one: we cut off the Hetwan attack, just like yesterday, only better. But that's not enough. I want the Hetwan down off the mountain. Which means a counterattack." He pointed at me. "Which means April's canyon. I'm going to take a force of three hundred men, veterans, down through the canyon. We're going to charge right into the main force down there and push them off the lowest plateau. With a little help from the air force."

"The air force?" Christopher echoed.

"Yeah," David said, managing a cocky John Wayne grin. "That would be the three of you. I have an idea. It's a one-shot kind of thing. Dangerous as hell, but Pegasus says he's up for it."

"Why is it that a horse is the most reliable character we've met on Olympus?" Christopher wondered.

"And me?" Senna asked. "What job do you have for me, General Davideus?"

"You? You passed as a Hetwan once. Do it again. Go and bring me one of the Coo-Hatch. We need to find out what it is that they want."

"You assume they want something?"

"Yeah. They're geniuses with metals, but they

don't know chemistry. Or didn't, until we traded them our chem book. Now they have gunpowder. But they're holding back. You think some little pop gun is all they can come up with? If you can build a rifle you can build a cannon. And instead of lead balls they could fire Coo-Hatch steel. Pass through anything. No, this isn't them trying to win a war, this is them trying to send a message. So let's talk to them." He nodded briskly, ending the discussion. "And now, let's move."

We fell into step behind him. Even Senna. I took some pleasure in seeing her reduced to obeying orders. But I knew in my heart that this détente would be short-lived.

She was right: She could dream big dreams here. She was right about it all. And for the first time I could really picture her not as some half-smart girl hanging around on the fringes of the adults' table trying to act clever, but as a real player. In Everworld there were greater powers by far. But not many with her combination of ruthless ambition and intelligence.

If David could be a general of the Greeks, Athena's hero, then maybe Senna could become the next Merlin. And more.

She'd left one thing off her litany of accomplishments: Even while trapped, even under threat from

Zeus and Athena, she had managed to lay a trap for Merlin that he would never suspect.

Merlin was subtle, but if he arrived at Olympus unprepared, he would be powerless to directly confront Zeus's power. He would walk in expecting to get a fair hearing, maybe convince Zeus to join his united front. Instead he'd be chained to a wall somewhere.

"Yeah, well, maybe he won't be so unprepared," I muttered under my breath. How I'd ever manage to warn Merlin, I didn't know. I hadn't seen the wizard since the battle with Loki at Galahad's castle.

I fought down a wave of futility. Senna had outsmarted us so far. She kept getting knocked down and kept popping right back up.

We marched outside. I felt a twinge of early homesickness. Not for my real home — that seemed too far away — but for this, our temporary home. It would be so nice to stay in bed and eat. So much better than what was coming next.

The horses were there, snorting and pawing the marble streets, ready to go. The chariot that had brought Senna was there, too.

David said, "Senna, you're on your own."

"What, no good-luck kiss?" she asked.

David jerked toward her, caught himself, and

withdrew, looking uncomfortable. To us he said, "Mount up and come with me. I'll show you what I need you to do."

I mounted Pelias's wing and settled onto his back. It wasn't that I was used to it, exactly, but now at least I trusted the flying horse not to drop me.

"To Hephaistos's workshop," David cried, and we were off, the four of us, flying through the air on horseback.

We flew northward, around the mountain, keeping our altitude this time. Almost around the back of the mountain I spotted what might have been a side vent of the volcano Olympus must once have been. It was a small crater, no bigger around than a circus tent. It glowed deep red.

We circled down toward that red glow. In the center of the crater there blazed a steaming pool of yellow magma. It might have been a lake of molten gold. The heat was intense as we flew far above it. The horses quickly sheered off and steered clear of the heat ripples for the rest of the descent.

All around the lake of liquid gold were workshops, not much different from the workshops we'd seen in villages down the mountain. They were crude wood-and-stone structures with hit-and-miss thatch roofs and open sides.

I could see firelit figures below, all working,

rushing here and there, or standing over rectangular fire pits that glowed red in counterpoint to the gold.

Down and down and suddenly we were landing in one of the few clear areas. Our arrival did not interrupt work. It did nothing to silence an incessant din of pounding, pounding hammers and sucking bellows and the hiss of white-hot metal being plunged into water.

It was like some medieval version of hell: fire and steam and swarthy, red-faced creatures in many shapes and sizes who could, at a casual glance, be taken for devils.

But this was the happiest place on Olympus. I saw dwarves, fairies, even a few trolls, and creatures I could only guess at. All looked sunburned, all wore minimal clothing and sweated from every pore, all were covered with soot, hair singed, eyebrows gone. Regardless of race or species, they showed massive hands with fingers that might have been made of thick tree roots.

They sang as they worked. They joked. They shouted crude insults at one another in raw voices. They laughed as they lifted hammers as big as their own heads, and carried bundles of still-smoking-hot swords, and manhandled big wicker baskets piled high with charcoal, and worked massive bellows that brought fires to white heat.

"Davideus!" a voice roared, a god's voice, no doubt about it. "It works. By Poseidon's moldy beard, it works."

Hephaistos, who I'd glimpsed only that once before, came rolling toward us, seated in a golden wheelchair. The wheelchair was a fantastic thing, all decorated with gold-and-silver horses' heads, sunbursts, and what looked an awful lot like a spear-launcher slung along the side. It had to weigh as much as a subcompact, but Hephaistos propelled it along almost effortlessly.

"You made improvements on my design," David said with a straight face, eyeing the decorations.

Hephaistos threw back his head and laughed. His body below the waist was of decidedly human proportions, tiny when contrasted with shoulders that would have intimidated a big gorilla. "All is in readiness, Davideus. The shipments of weapons have gone out, but as you see, we keep busy preparing more."

"And our special project?"

"All ready," the immortal said with a wink. He pointed with his beard toward where a team of his blacksmiths were attaching strange harnesses to Pelias and his two brothers.

"Good. Then I have to go. The Hetwan are on the march," David said. "Will you show my friends what they need to do?" Without waiting for an answer David said, "Jalil, Christopher, April, Hephaistos will tell you what to do. But the hard part is knowing when to strike. I'll be on the ground, in April's canyon. We need a one-two punch. My boys and I attack. Then, just as we engage, just after the Hetwan turn to come for us, you hit their rear."

"Hit them with what?" Jalil asked peevishly.

"You'll see," David said, already walking away and calling to Pegasus.

"That is as happy as you are ever going to see David," Christopher said. "He's simultaneously channeling Napoleon, Patton, and Robert E. Lee from beyond the grave."

"Come," Hephaistos said cheerily and swung his absurd wheelchair around.

Ten minutes later we knew. And we were none of us happy.

"Oh, this is a good idea," Christopher said as we climbed up on our mounts.

"Remember," Hephaistos called to us, "the ropes must be cut in sequence. Number one, then number two and three at the exact same moment or else the weight will drag you down."

"Yeah, I think we have a pretty clear mental picture of that," Jalil said.

"This is just great," Christopher muttered.

David's plan had several major ways to go

wrong. Ways that might kill us, or kill our allies. It had only one way to actually work.

Hephaistos had built a vast, deep pot. A pot you might use to cook half a dozen cows. The pot was set into a brass ring. Three padded ropes led from the ring and attached to special harnesses fitted to our three horses.

It was, of course, impossible that the horses could lift the pot. But then it was impossible that they could fly at all. And somehow Hephaistos had determined, to his own satisfaction at least, that the three winged horses could carry their burden — but not a pound more.

If the weight of the pot became unbalanced it would drag the horses down. And us. It might even end up with the three winged horses and us, their riders, spinning, falling, tumbling out of control through the air as the contents of the pot tumbled with us.

The content of the pot was fire. Glowing red embers from every forge in the crater. Red-hot coals. A thousand backyard barbecues' worth of black-and-red charcoal briquettes.

We were going to firebomb the Hetwan.

XVIII

We flew. I don't know how, but we flew.

The horses were straining, bathed in sweat, wings beating far faster than usual. Pelias had no time to spare for conversation. And his tension spread all too easily to me.

We flew, and the massive pot swayed slowly between us as the horses held to a fixed pattern, as precise as the Blue Angels at an air show.

If one of them flew even a few feet too low the weight would shift and this airborne house of cards would fall.

We said nothing, the three of us. No one wanted to distract the horses. No one wanted to even pretend that we weren't scared to death.

One of Hephaistos's dwarves, who it turned out came from Norse country, had fixed a short sword and scabbard around my waist. It was to cut the rope and drop the fire.

We flew in a triangle, with Christopher on point. He would cut his rope first. That would tip the pot forward, unbalance it. It would also slam Jalil and me with too much weight. So we had to time our cuts to the second. The pot had to tip. But only very slightly, because if we waited, our horses' wings would buckle and we'd all fall to our deaths.

And we had to cut at the precise same instant. We'd worked out a signal. Christopher would yell, "Cut!" when he made his downward slash.

On that cue, as fast we could, Jalil and I would cut. There would be a slight delay as our brains absorbed Christopher's cry and reacted. We could only hope that Jalil and I would delay and respond at almost the identical speed.

And of course we'd want to do all this over the heads of the Hetwan, not over the Greeks.

Below us, down on the ground that now seemed so far away and so safe, the battle was joined. The Hetwan were climbing their lattice-work of steps and ladders uphill to the second plateau. The Greeks met them, steel against burning venom.

But a pair of wheeled catapults had been moved forward to a position just behind the

Greek line. The structures themselves were three times the height of a man. A tall A-frame supported an arm that was half as long as the frame and had a massive wooden basket filled with rocks on one end and a small basket on the other.

Brawny soldiers turned a spoked wheel that raised the counterweight and lowered the basket. When the basket was chest-high it was filled with a porous volcanic rock that had been soaked in coal oil. Just before the launch a soldier would thrust a torch into the basket. The rock would flame and, at a yelled order, the counterweight would be released.

The burning missile drew a red-and-black arc through the air and fell toward the Hetwan steps.

All this, we saw from a distance. Our target was farther down the mountain, down on the lowest of the plateaus. It was from this lowest plateau that the Hetwan were launching the attack.

The horses began their descent. Slowly. So carefully. Turning and dropping and turning again, straining every muscle, foam forming around their mouths, eyes staring, wild.

Down. Down till we were at the same altitude as the main battle, and now the catapult missiles seemed to be aimed right at us. They would arc high, then drop toward us. And no chance, no slight chance of moving to avoid them.

I gritted my teeth. David had made a mistake. He'd overlooked this. Understandable. He wasn't exactly straight from the ancient Greek version of West Point; he wasn't a real general. Mistakes happened in wars, always had. But I was furious anyway. I wasn't feeling generous. I wasn't in a forgiving mood.

I could only see that the catapult missiles would plunge down on one of us, come whistling and smoking down on us and we would fall to our deaths.

One was coming. Coming. Arcing high, falling . . . right at me. Right at me. It would hit me, oh, God, I'd die, oh, God.

The flaming boulder blew past me, between me and the fiery pot. It missed the rope, missed me. But the smoke rolled over me and I choked and gagged and tried not to move a millimeter as I gasped for breath lest I upset Pelias's equilibrium.

I called David some names, silently under my breath, but with terrifying fury. Had to have someone to blame.

But now we were safely beyond the arc of the flaming missiles. They fell behind us as we dropped slowly along the slope, now actually beneath the level of the main battle.

We were flying level with the climbing, scaling

Hetwan. I could see the damage the catapults were doing. Several small fires had taken hold.

But I could see that this time the Hetwan were better prepared. There were bucket brigades of Hetwan carrying small bottles of water that they passed from weak hand to weak hand and spilled on the fire.

Too little, but better for them than nothing. It was an effort, at least, and it might slow the spread of fire.

Spread below us was the lowest plateau, the bottom step of the mountain. It was covered, every square inch, by close-pressed Hetwan. They'd learned this lesson, too. Yesterday they'd been unprepared to follow up and throw more warriors into the fight. Not today. These Hetwan were poised, ready to push ahead, ready to keep up the assault, regardless of losses.

"They learn," I muttered to myself. "They're new at this, like David said, but they do learn."

My eye was drawn to a sudden movement. Around the mountain, the canyon invisible to the Hetwan began to spit forth men in armor.

I saw David clearly, no helmet on his head, but with Galahad's sword held high. He was yelling and running all out, through the rocks, around the stunted trees, scrambling with an ever-growing force at his back.

The Hetwan reacted slowly. It wasn't till David's men hit the edge of the plateau and began hacking into the surprised Hetwan that the aliens at last turned to face this unexpected threat.

There were easily five thousand Hetwan on the plateau. David's force looked ridiculous, pathetic. They were outnumbered ten, fifteen, maybe twenty to one. The Hetwan would crush them by sheer weight of numbers.

Unless.

Christopher's horse was in front. We wheeled through the sky, observed from below but unchallenged. We turned, a slow, clumsy, triangular Frisbee, and came sweeping far over the heads of David's men.

Now we were over the Hetwan. Every muscle in my body was rigid. I drew out the short sword. My palm sweated and slicked the handle. If I dropped it . . . My fingers cramped tight.

"Ready!" Christopher yelled and I almost didn't know what he meant. My brain was buzzing, weirded, my senses all sped up and slowed down and strange to me.

I raised my sword. Glanced at Jalil. He did not look at me.

"Cut!"

Too soon! I wasn't ready!

Slash. Down, cut, cut. I felt the blade hit the rope.

Saw Christopher's rope twang with sudden release. Saw the slightest forward-tipping of the pot.

Saw Jalil's rope snap like a bridge cable under too much pressure.

My blade. Bounced! Hit, cut, but not through, not through and a jolt like we'd been hit by a train. All the weight yanked down on Pelias.

He was jerked onto his side. Right wing collapsed as his left wing beat pointlessly, driving us down. I was off his back. Legs in the air. Nothing to hold, nothing but air.

Chapter
XIX

Midair. Falling. Bare legs kicking at nothing.

The tight rope slapped against me, like being whipped. It caught me across the chest. A shock of pain. Wind knocked out of me.

Up down and down up and nothing where it should be, I slashed, slashed, not cutting, just desperate, just panic — thinking that maybe my sword would grab something solid.

I felt the resistance as my blade hit the taut rope. And the sudden release as it cut through.

The burning pot was spinning away below me, spraying its red-hot contents in a shower, a Roman candle of blazing sparks.

Wham! A wing hit me in the back. I grabbed at something, nothing. Hand closed on air.

Something brushed my leg. And in a freak accident of good timing or luck or the Holy Mother's swift answer to a babbled prayer, my ankle was wrapped and caught by recoiling rope.

The rope was attached to Pelias, and he caught the air in his impossible wings and I wasn't falling.

I twisted up and grabbed rope just as my ankle came loose. I hung by one hand. An idiot trapeze act. A daredevil madwoman not just tempting fate but spitting in its face and daring it to kill her.

I swung, my own sneakers mere inches from the heads of the Hetwan, the Hetwan who were running and spinning and screaming their inhuman screams as the fire from the sky burned into them.

My grip slipped. I slid down the rope. Rope burn tore at my palm. But I hit a knot, and that saved me. My hand jammed against the knot, I swung madly, no longer above the Hetwan but down through them, a pendulum passing swiftly through rows of pain-maddened aliens.

All around me blurred insect faces, mouth-parts, shrieks, reaching hands. In front, blocked! I was going to hit him, run into him. I'd be knocked loose and I would burn as they were burning all around me!

I hit dirt. Half running, half dragged, my legs scraped over dirt and dying Hetwan and searing coals.

"Oh, God, help me!" I cried.

Lower still, as Pelias, exhausted, fought futilely to lift me. Two Hetwan fell on me, ready to smother me if that's what it took to kill me. They rushed at me and I stabbed with my short sword as the coals I had dropped now burned into my knees and I screamed with pain and knew I was going to die and shrieked in agony, "Athena! Help me!"

The Hetwan closed on me but I was no longer there. I was in the air, sliding through their grasp. Flying. Pelias had lifted me.

With God's help.

Or Athena's.

Chapter XX

Pelias pulled me up and away, swiftly now, and Jalil was swinging in beside me. His horse moved under me, rose to meet me, and then Jalil's welcome, blessed arms were around my waist, pulling me down, holding me tightly.

I was shaking.

"That was close," Jalil said.

"Did you see?" I croaked. "Was it her? Was it Athena?"

I could feel him shaking his head. "I didn't see anything, except it looked like your horse caught a headwind maybe and got some lift."

Of course, I thought. Of course. The obvious answer. The sensible, twenty-first-century-American answer. No God. And no god. It didn't matter that I had called to her, that in that awful moment of terror I had trusted Athena to save me, but had not trusted my own God.

Logical, that's all it was. Athena had saved me before. She'd lifted me up out of danger, of course I called to her, of course. That wasn't blasphemy, I wasn't saying she was a true god, I wasn't trading the God I'd prayed to all my life for some seven-foot-tall immortal in a battle helmet.

Athena, help me.

"Come on," Jalil said gently, "we'll head back home."

"No. This isn't over." I looked down at the ground. We were high above the lower plateau, but too low still to see up onto the higher plateau.

Down beneath us the Hetwan burned alive. They seemed lost. Wandering, shrieking, slapping at the fires that burned them. The hard part of my soul thought they were getting a taste of their own medicine. I still felt the pain of yesterday, of Hetwan venom burning into my stomach, sizzling the fat, nibbling into me, a fire rat eating its way inside me.

The hard part of me thought, *Burn. Burn, you murderous, evil insects*.

But part of me, too, was horrified. They seemed strangely helpless. As though this problem had simply never come up before. Some slapped at the fire, some brushed it away. But Hetwan flesh, if that's what it's called, does burn. Some of the Hetwan were completely engulfed, walking, stumbling pillars of fire.

They seemed unable to organize, unable to figure out what to do next. And David's men were slaughtering them, almost unopposed.

Suddenly, out of the sky, Christopher swooped low above the Hetwan horde. In a voice that carried all the way to Jalil and me he yelled, "Run! Run away, you damned stupid fools! Run away!"

It was absurd, of course. Silly even. Misplaced humor. Jalil started to laugh. Then he stopped himself and whispered, "No, he's right. He's right. Look."

And just then a shock wave spread through the Hetwan. A ripple, as though they were a burning lake and someone had tossed in a boulder. All at once, they were running. Slidey-glideying off the plateau, stumbling as quickly as they could down the steps and stairs and onto the more manageable slopes below.

It wasn't panic. It wasn't that they were terrified. It was, as Christopher had somehow intuited, that till then they had not known what to do. They had not known how to respond when they were burned from the sky and slashed from the side. That wasn't in the game plan, and they had wandered, confused and lost till someone told them what to do.

Till Christopher had told them to run.

They ran. They flew. They panicked without ever seeming to feel a moment of actual fear.

We rose up on a warm pillar created by burning Hetwan bodies. Up till we could peek over the rim of the second plateau. Here the Hetwan were hemmed in, trapped between wings of the Greek army. David's men, having won below, were coming up the hill, fighting gravity and the smoke from the burning Hetwan stairs to hit the remaining Hetwan from a third side.

In the middle of the encircled Hetwan I spotted two Coo-Hatch adults. The two Coo-Hatch were standing over their gun, guarding it. They, at least, were scared.

"Look! Look at that Hetwan," I said to Jalil and pointed.

A Hetwan was forcing its way through his fellows with unusual individual purpose. And he was carrying a very human-style dagger.

"It's Senna," Jalil said.

"She's trying to get the Coo-Hatch out of there."

"No. She's going to kill them."

"What?"

David had told her to bring at least one of the Coo-Hatch out alive. That was the order. Not to assassinate them.

"No!" I cried.

Senna drew back her arm, keeping the knife low and out of sight, and stabbed one of the Coo-Hatch. The knife went in only a couple of inches, so she leaned her weight into it and the Coo-Hatch cried out and staggered.

"Down!" Jalil roared to his horse, and we plunged.

The Coo-Hatch fell, trying to reach one of its larger arms around to feel the wound. The other Coo-Hatch gaped, amazed and puzzled. But all he saw were Hetwan.

Senna had the knife behind her back. I lost her for a moment in the press of bodies, but then she was there again, almost within reach of the remaining Coo-Hatch.

The Greeks were surging, cutting through the Hetwan with renewed vigor now that David and his men had joined them. But Senna would reach the Coo-Hatch before the Greeks did.

"Do you see that Hetwan, the one with the knife?" Jalil asked his horse.

"Yes."

"Can you hit her . . . can you hit him in the head with your hooves?"

The horse made no answer. And I had to fight down an improbable, knee-jerk concern for my half sister. I hated her. Despised her. And did not want her badly injured.

Down we went, swooped into level flight, fast as an eagle on the attack. I felt a thump vibrate up through the horse's body. We zoomed past, turned sharply, and I saw the Hetwan with the knife was gone. In his place lay Senna, unconscious, the knife several feet away.

In moments the Greeks swept the Hetwan back from Senna, back from the dead Coo-Hatch. I saw three warriors seize the surviving, unresisting Coo-Hatch roughly and hold him at sword point. Then David was there, standing over Senna.

He knelt down, moved to pick her up. Then, without touching her, got to his feet again and took a step back.

"Good boy," I whispered.

Chapter
XXI

This time we did not go to see Zeus. Zeus, we were informed, had spent the day getting roaring drunk and was back in eagle form, flying south to look for maidens. Dionysus had the party in full, manic swing. Zeus's temple was a frat house.

Christopher said, "So, his people are down there getting killed, fighting for his sorry ass all day long, and he's out looking for a good time. Perfect."

No one spoke up in defense of Father Zeus.

Instead we crawled exhausted back to Motel 6 Olympus, dragged our bodies back to our rooms, and fell into our separate beds. Senna was locked in a room. David handed his sword to one of the servants and told him to use it on Senna if she tried to get out.

I expected to be asleep in an instant. But my

head was buzzing. Too tired to sleep. Questions. Nothing but questions.

Why had Senna killed the Coo-Hatch? How was I ever going to warn Merlin? Why did I care?

Had Athena saved me? Had God saved me? Was it necessary to even wonder — didn't God have a hand in everything, even in the actions of a . . . of whatever Athena was?

But that wasn't it, and I knew it. That wasn't the question. The question was, why had I called to her? Why had I called to Athena?

The answer was bitter to me. And obvious. Because I had seen her. Because she was real. No faith necessary, Athena was real.

I drifted into sleep. I crossed. And even there, there in the real world, there were David and Jalil and Christopher. The four of us were huddling in a cold wind outside the cafeteria. I could see all the kids inside eating. But I knew that David had signaled to me to join him outside, and so there I was. Out where we could have privacy. And be cold.

"We need to figure out what to say to Athena about Senna and the Coo-Hatch," David said.

Jalil and David had been here for a few minutes longer than I. Christopher had shown up just after me. I was still adjusting, still absorbing the day's news from Everworld. The images and emotions, the memories so real, so vivid that I found I was checking myself for the wounds I'd left over there, on a different/same body.

"Athena may already know," Jalil cautioned. "If she does, and we lie, she could turn on us in a flash."

"She may hurt Senna," David said, sounding as neutral as he could and fooling neither of us.

"This is kind of pointless, isn't it?" I wondered. "You know? For all we know, we're already awake back there. The Everworld us may be awake again, and we may just be real worlders, and the other Jalil and the other David and the other me may have already made the decisions."

David looked blank, annoyed. Jalil let a small smile appear and disappear.

"What's funny?" I asked him sharply.

"We've become the subset," he said.

I knew what he meant. Or thought I did.

"What's that supposed to mean?" David asked.

Jalil shrugged and hitched his coat collar up to block a fresh wind. "Started out the Everworld us were a part of the real-world us. We were real, they were . . . I don't know. Not so real. We were real life, they were characters on TV. They, over there, they worried about how to get back here. Now we, over here, just wonder what's going on over there. We wait for the updates. The more that happens over there, the smaller our lives here seem to us. They're getting bigger, and we're getting smaller."

My heart sank as he talked. I wanted to deny it. But how could I? And what's the point in denying the truth?

"There's not much point in our making decisions here, April's right," Christopher said. "We war-game here, maybe the decisions are already made back over there."

"Well, what are we supposed to do?" David demanded. "Just go back inside and eat the lousy veggie lasagna? We're in the middle of a war here."

Jalil shook his head. "No. We're in the middle of a war there. No war here. No gods. You don't even have a sword, David. We're just April O'Brien and David Levin and Jalil Sherman. And Christopher Hitchcock, except he must have skipped class today.

"See, you were actually the first to get it, David. You knew instinctively that Everworld was going to eat us up. So you went for it. I admire that kind of intuition. You knew, way back when we were on that Viking ship and you were running off about 'What's so great about the real world, what's it ever going to do for us.' You embraced the inevitable."

"Screw you, Jalil," I said. I started for the door back inside. But I stopped. "I get so sick of your smug, know-it-all crap. You're always just too cool, aren't you? Always about two steps away, not quite involved. It's all just this interesting play to you. You clap politely when something interesting happens. But you're never exactly on the stage yourself."

"I am who I am," he said. Only the lower tone of his voice gave any indication that I'd gotten to him.

"So am I!" I yelled. "I am who I am. I'm going to stay who I am. This is me. Here. This person, with this brain, this heart, these ideas, my friends, my family, even this depressing school. My hopes, my dreams, which by the way do not include being Joan of Arc for a bunch of lunatic so-called gods. I'm not letting Everworld change me."

Jalil didn't answer. He just looked down at the ground. As though I'd said something embarrassing. As though I'd made a fool of myself and he didn't want to witness my embarrassment.

I was red in the face. I could feel it. It didn't matter. I was right.

David said, "Well, all that was very interesting, but we still should think about what to tell Athena." He held up a hand to silence my objection. "Even if we are already back there, maybe we're not, and this is a big issue. What to tell them about Senna and the Coo-Hatch."

Through the window I saw Magda and 'Suela and Alison laughing and picking at their food. Talking about guys. About acting. About clothes, movies, music, TV, the teachers. They were saving a place for me.

"We can't lie," Jalil said. "Not when Athena may already know the truth."

I should go back in. My friends expected me. I should go back in.

Instead I said, "Jalil's right. And it's not what Senna will expect, which makes it even more right. She still has in her head that we're her allies in some way. Like we're on the same team. We need to . . ."

That was the last of what I remembered, the last few words that stuck in my brain as I woke up and threw the covers off in frustration.

"What?" I accused the servant who'd shaken me.

"The goddess Athena calls for your presence."

Chapter

XXII

Athena's temple, or palace or whatever it was, was a bit less grandiose than Zeus's. In fact, she met us in a sort of library. There were tall, rolled manuscripts displayed upright on shelves or stacked flat in cubbyholes that stretched from waist height all the way to the painted ceiling far overhead.

Thousands of books, I suppose they were. And massive stone tables placed just like you'd expect in some ancient version of a public library.

The four of us plus Senna were there. So was the surviving Coo-Hatch. This time, his juvenile-phase counterpart was there, flitting around in a highly caffeinated way.

Athena sat on a modest chair without a platform and, for the first time, unarmed. There was a large canvas bag at her feet.

"My father is occupied," she said dryly. "It falls

to me to hear from this Coo-Hatch creature. And to hear your reports of the great victory. Speak, Coo-Hatch. Why have you sold your magic to the Hetwan? Why have you come against Olympus, which has never done you harm?"

The Coo-Hatch glanced at me. Was it the very Coo-Hatch to whom I'd handed our chemistry book what seemed like aeons ago?

"We do not make war on Olympus," the Coo-Hatch said.

Athena reached down and with a flick of her fingers tore open the bag. The Coo-Hatch gun lay there.

"This is some cunning instrument for killing at a distance. Do you deny it is yours?"

"We have made it," the Coo-Hatch said proudly. "And we could make many more, and far more powerful. Powerful enough to batter down the very walls of Olympus itself."

"You lie!" Athena snapped.

"He's telling the truth," David said. "Cannons could be built. They could be used to fire cannonballs . . . like, um, like boulders. As fast as Zeus's thunderbolts. And just as far.

"Of course," David added, "they could also be placed around the rim of Ka Anor's crater, where they could blow his city, his home apart."

The Coo-Hatch said nothing.

Athena nodded. "I see. Friend Coo-Hatch bargains. He shows us his strength and offers to sell his loyalty."

"Coo-Hatch do not serve Ka Anor," the strange alien said. "Neither do they serve Olympus. Coo-Hatch serve the Coo-Hatch."

"So your filthy gods sent you to attack us?" Athena demanded.

"The god of the fire and the goddess of the ore have not sent us. It was the god of the fire and goddess of the ore who brought us here, against our will, to this universe, far from our forges and families. The Coo-Hatch will revere the god of the fire who taught us the ways of the steel, and the goddess of the ore, who first showed us the sacred metals. But we will no longer serve them."

"You rebel against the gods?" Athena was outraged. As outraged, it seemed to me, as if they had been Greeks rebelling against her.

"Coo-Hatch be free," the Coo-Hatch said. "We go home. In peace, if can be. If no way is found to return in peace to our forges and mines, Coo-Hatch will harm all the gods of Everworld until one shall let us go."

I saw Jalil nodding. He was watching the Coo-Hatch with shrewd appreciation.

"This Coo-Hatch is threatening all the gods," Senna said, speaking for the first time. "If mere mortals are allowed to abandon the gods, if they are free to fear or not fear their rightful gods, then what must happen?"

The argument hit home with Athena. I could see that. Her expression hardened. Her eyes were angry.

"A traitor to his own gods today is a traitor to all the gods tomorrow," Senna pressed.

"If the Coo-Hatch go back to their own universe, they will be a threat to no one," Jalil argued.

I looked at my half sister. I watched her watching Athena. Jalil's argument had made no impact on the goddess of wisdom and war.

I knew what to say. I knew now why Senna had murdered the other Coo-Hatch. But what would Athena do? She might well kill Senna. Right here and now. Right in front of me. The question was: Was Athena as smart and pragmatic as she seemed? Or was she just another power-mad crazy?

David was right. We should have spent our real-world time figuring this out.

"Senna may be telling the truth," I said. "But she has her own reasons. Wise Athena, this witch, my sister, killed the other Coo-Hatch and would have killed this one."

Senna failed to control herself. She blazed with pure hatred.

"Senna is a gateway," I continued. "At least Loki thinks so. Maybe she could open an escape path for the Coo-Hatch, back to their own universe. She doesn't want to. But maybe she could."

The Coo-Hatch began to tremble. Anger that Senna had killed his compatriot? Or excitement at the possibility that he had found his escape?

"I killed the other Coo-Hatch," Senna said coldly. The rage was banked, no longer blazing. Still there. "But I cannot help the Coo-Hatch. If I gave my life, became a mere tool, yes, I could open a path to the old world. But I don't have the power to open a doorway to a universe I've never inhabited."

"So why kill the Coo-Hatch?" I asked.

And Athena said, "Answer carefully, witch. Your life hangs by a gossamer thread and I hold the blade."

Senna didn't answer her directly. She laughed ruefully and shook her head and said to herself, "Had to be. There was no avoiding it. Not over the long haul."

"Speak!" Athena roared in a voice that rattled the walls as effectively as her father's bellow.

"There is another who has the power," Senna said. "A witch of older and greater powers than mine. She serves Isis. Here in Everworld. She has

vowed never to use her power except . . . She has
vowed never to use her power. But she may be
able to do this thing the Coo-Hatch demands."

"Name this witch," Athena said.

"My mother," Senna said.

EVER WORLD

#

BRAVE THE BETRAYAL

The mud was a living thing, a murderous force. It forced me down, pushed me, rolled over me, covered me, smothered me, lifted me and swept me away.

It was in my nose, eyes, ears, mouth. It billowed beneath my clothing, squeezed into my shoes. I weighed a thousand pounds. I moved like a man asleep, I moved like a slow-motion special effect, swimming in pudding.

I held my breath, lungs burning, tried to spit the stuff out of my mouth only to have the pressure of the mud fill my mouth further and threaten to force its way down my throat to clog my lungs and bloat my stomach.

All at once I was atop the wave, floating, uplifted on a rushing river of mud. I was a bit of bark tossed along on the rushing stream, not sinking but threatening to be swallowed up by ripples and currents and eddies.

Down a tunnel. Through the bowels of the earth, racing beneath a low rock ceiling, and then, all at once, sunlight!

The ground vomited me up and I was turned around, lost, dazed, upended. I had the illusion that the mud flow was suddenly above me, that it was flying over my head, even though I was still in it, still stuck in the goo.

I felt I had to grab onto the mud, had to clutch at it to keep from flying straight down into the sky.

Then, the mud washed me up, like a murderous tsunami that in the end comes to little more than a rush of foam on the sand. I was a beaten, barely-survived surfer, staggering up/down, falling, no falling upward, what was happening?

The sky, bright Clorox white and flecked with blue clouds, was below me, under my head. I was standing but my feet couldn't possibly stick to the ground, couldn't, could not, because I knew that it was all upside down.

I felt the sky beneath me. I saw the sun, black and yet bright, shining in a white sky, peeking around baby blue clouds.

"What the holy crap is going on?!" Christopher yelled.

I saw him, like me, seemingly glued to a ground that had become a ceiling. I cringed, knelt, tried to fight the absurd urge to grab onto the ground, to clutch big handfuls of the royal blue grass.

I fought it. Impossible. The ground had to be below me, the sky had to be above. *Don't be stupid, Jalil, you're not falling toward the sky. Gravity is still toward the ground, that hasn't changed.*

But everything had changed. I was in danger of falling straight down into a sky as white as a blank page. I could fall into the black sun.

I saw the others. Each covered in filth, each dragging themselves up or crawling or cringing, all looking fearfully at the sky below, all holding, or wanting to hold onto the ground itself lest they fly off.

I closed my eyes. That was the way. That was it, the only way to fight the illusion. Blinded, I could keep from throwing up. Blinded I could believe everything was where it should be.

"Close your eyes," I croaked, spitting mud. "It helps. Close your eyes."

"Okay, my eyes are closed," Christopher said. "Now someone tell me what the hell is going on here? What is this, Alice in Wonder-freaking-land? Where's the big white rabbit? Where's the caterpillar with the hookah? 'Cause absolutely nothing is going to make this any weirder."

David, his voice shaky, but trying to project whatever stability and sanity he could manage, asked me. "Jalil, man, you get this?"

"No, I don't," I said shortly. "I feel like I'm upside down. Or else like everything else is. I know gravity is holding me to the ground but I can't lose the feeling that the ground is up and the sky is down."

I pried my drying-mud-caked eyes and peeked again. The illusion came back full force. I heard someone puking, but that was the last thing I needed to see: vomit falling down into the sky. Although, no, it would fall to the ground.

"It's a sight thing," I said. "I mean I feel that down is down. My arms aren't trying to relax toward the sky." I tried a small jump, feeling idiotic. A small jump, just to see whether I fell into the sky. I landed on the ground.

"It's a sight thing," I repeated more confidently, but with my eyes closed for sanity's sake.

"It's a reverse image," April said. She sounded close. "It's not just the upside-down thing. The sky is the color of clouds and the clouds are the color of sky. The sun is black, not white or yellow. The grass is blue. It's all the reverse, all the opposite."

"White sky is not the reverse of blue sky," I said, sounding pedantic even to myself. "Black sun is not the opposite of a yellow sun. Blue grass is not —"

"Stop being literal," April interrupted excitedly. "It's not science, it's . . . it's poetry. Poetic opposites. I mean, whoever came up with this didn't know about the light spectrum. They just thought 'what would be the opposite of whatever?'"

"Yeah," David agreed dubiously. "It's opposite world or whatever."

True enough, I thought. Yes, not a scientist's idea of opposites. A simpler mind. Less concerned with abstract notions of truth and accuracy. Not a modern vision, an older one.

"It's the gods," I said disgustedly. "It's right about their level of thinking: primitive. Irrational. Inconsistent."

I was surprised to hear Senna laugh. "You just don't ever learn, do you Jalil? You really think this is a good time to be insulting the gods?"

"I gotta go with the witch on this," Christopher muttered. "I'm thinking next time someone says, 'kill a sheep for the gods,' just kill the sheep. Crazy mothers want a dead sheep, let's give them a dead sheep."

"It's a mirror world," Senna mused. "A subtle notion of an afterlife, don't you think? The details are inconsistent, but it was a fascinating idea."

"Hey, let's stand around on our heads and admire it all," Christopher said shrilly. "Senna and Jalil and April, you three can lead the discussion. Me, I'm going to grab onto this dirt so I don't fall off the earth and go flying off into space."

"What do we do?" April asked.

"I don't know," David admitted. "This is . . . new. Can't get back where we want to be, the tunnel or hole or whatever, is all plugged up with mud. No way back through there."

Senna said, "Well, well, finally a situation where Mighty Davideus admits he's lost."

"You have a plan, Senna?" Christopher snapped, coming to David's defense.

"Yes, actually. Let's find a stream and get washed off."

"How are we supposed to walk anywhere?" April demanded.

Senna laughed, a surprisingly happy sound. "It's hard for you, isn't it? The four of you, so normal and conventional underneath it all." She spread her arms wide. "It's magic, boys and girl. Magic! Welcome to my world."

She didn't quite twirl around in girlish delight, but she looked like she wanted to.

"We do have to get this mud off us before we end up baked solid," I said. "There must be water, or something like it."

"Yeah, let's all find a nice bath," Christopher agreed. "And by the way, if anyone sees a sheep, fold your Ten Commandments and your Constitution and stick them right up your butt, then kill the damn sheep."